LAKEHOUSE DREAMS

JODI ALLEN BRICE

For my family. Your support of my dreams means everything.

CHAPTER 1

*S*arah Williams narrowed her eyes, as the bright stage lights shone directly on her.

She ran her hands down the sides of her sleeveless white silk dress embellished with Swarovski crystals. Not her usual style, she tended to gravitate to Boho chic, but this wasn't her usual bar singing gig. This was the big time.

Sarah couldn't see the crowd in front of her, but she knew they were there. She could sense them.

A male cleared their throat in the front row. The scent of expensive perfume wafted in from the right. A couple of murmurs rose up from the back of the audience. A shush drifted down from the balcony.

Her stomach knotted with butterflies, then slowly relaxed as the band behind started playing the familiar song she'd sung a thousand times.

Sarah took a deep breath and slowly let it out. Her hand drifted to the microphone in front of her.

It was time to shine.

She leaned into the microphone and opened her mouth to sing the words of the song she'd written a few months ago.

Every nerve in her body tingled as she sang the chorus, each one filled with an emotion of sadness and longing and loss.

The notes rose higher and higher until she finished the song in a crescendo.

The second the song ended, the audience she couldn't see stood to their feet in thunderous applause.

When the spotlight dimmed, she could finally view the looks on her adoring fans.

The stadium was full, not an empty seat in the house.

All for her.

They were all there for her.

She heard an annoying buzzing sound to the left of the stage. She attempted to ignore it, so she could enjoy the moment, but the more she tried, the louder the noise became.

Angrily, she reached her arm out and slammed her hand on something hard.

Sarah blinked, opened her eyes, and then realized the annoying sound was her phone ringing.

She groaned. It wasn't real. It was all just a dream.

She sat up in bed and glanced at the clock.

Six o'clock. Who the heck calls at six in the freaking morning?

She accidentally kicked her guitar, and the pages of

music she'd been working on late last night, onto the floor.

Groaning, she picked up her phone.

Candy Ryan.

Candy was the mother of Ben. Her little brother Johnny and Ben were best friends. What in the world did she want so early?

She hit the answer call button and pressed it to her ear.

"Hello?"

"Sarah, this is Dennis Ryan, Candy's husband. I'm so sorry to call you this early."

"That's okay." It really wasn't okay, but she didn't have the energy to be rude.

"I'm calling from my wife's phone because I don't have your number. Anyway, Candy can't take Johnny to school today. Her father passed away last night, and she is packing to go to her mom's to help with funeral arrangements."

Sarah straightened in bed. "Oh, I'm so sorry to hear that."

"I just wanted to call you before we left so you'd know you would have to take and pick up Johnny for at least the next week. I'm not sure when we'll be back."

"Oh, okay. Well, thank you for calling me. And tell Candy I'm sorry for her loss."

"Thanks, Sarah, I will."

She ended the call and tossed her phone on the bed. Reality soaked in.

Sarah wasn't a superstar, and people were not clamoring to hear her sing.

She wasn't even traveling around, singing at dive bars while she roamed across America in her remodeled van.

She was here, in Hopeton, North Carolina, raising her eight-year-old brother, Johnny, after her parents' tragic death, and trying to keep it together.

It had only been a few months since that fateful day when her parent died in a plane crash. They'd been on a mission trip to Costa Rica, helping with an orphanage when their small plane crashed.

She had been in Oregon when she'd gotten the news from her parents' attorney.

Upon learning of the crash, Sarah had gotten into her van and driven two days, stopping only to rest her eyes a while before continuing on.

With the help of her attorney and the American government, they'd gotten the bodies back into the States within a week.

She barely remembered the funeral, and had been in survival mode ever since.

At twenty-eight, the last thing Sarah expected in life was to be stuck in a small town, with people she couldn't even connect with, while raising a kid.

Yet here she was.

CHAPTER 2

*S*arah walked into the kitchen in her boxer shorts and the T-shirt she'd slept in. She headed straight to the coffeemaker and began fixing a pot. Her mom was a sucker for 'if it's not broke, don't fix it', she had never upgraded their coffee pot. Not that Sarah minded. She'd spent many mornings in the middle of nowhere making coffee over a campfire. She didn't care about fancy coffees. As long as she got her daily infusion of caffeine, she was happy.

While the coffee began brewing, she glanced around the kitchen where she'd spent a majority of her childhood. Her mother never painted the old oak cabinets or updated the tile countertops. They had painted the walls a soft gray, the only update she'd noticed since her last visit home, before her….

Just thinking about her parents' death made her chest ache.

She should have visited more often, called more

often. Maybe if she had, then she would feel closer to Johnny.

Sarah remembered when she was a senior in high school, her parents telling her they had amazing news. She was going to be a sister.

Instead of elated, she'd felt sick to her stomach. Her parents were in their forties and had never, ever said anything about wanting another baby. The worst part, because of the new baby, they would not be able to send her to Europe for her graduation present. They were going to have to use that money to upgrade their car to a new SUV for the baby.

She'd been angry, but most of all, hurt by their betrayal.

Sarah had never asked for much from them, but she had been counting on that trip.

Instead of wallowing in self-pity, she did the only thing she could. She took the money she'd saved working odd jobs for the last three years and bought a used van. During her senior year, while her friends were going to parties on the weekend, she was remodeling her vehicle. She was going to make it into a home where she could travel and see America. When she was done, the van had a functioning kitchen, a small sitting area, and a bed. The day after graduating, she took off in her van to the west coast, two days after her brother's birth.

Her gaze landed on a photograph of her and her parents before Johnny had come along.

They took it at the beach when Sarah had turned

twelve. A stranger had taken the picture while she and her parents posed in front of the sunset over the ocean. It was the first real vacation she'd ever been on. And it was the first time that she caught a taste of wanderlust.

A crashing sound erupted above her head where Johnny's bedroom was.

She hurried to the bottom of the stairs and called up, "Everything okay?"

"Yeah. Some books fell out of my bookcase."

Sarah relaxed and headed back into the kitchen, where she placed a box of cereal, a white bowl and the quart of milk on the small kitchen table.

Johnny straggled into the kitchen and eased into the kitchen chair.

"You need to hurry and eat before we leave for school."

Johnny looked up at her with a scowl. "You're not taking me to school, are you?"

"Yes. Ben's father called and said they had a family emergency and had to go out of town." She poured herself another cup of coffee and laced it heavily with cream and sugar. She stood at the window and looked out over Laurel Lake, afraid if she'd sit down, she'd be tempted not to get up. What she'd give if she could climb back into bed and pull the covers over her head.

"So, Ben won't be at school either?" Her little brother looked up at her with wide eyes.

"No. They had a death in the family." Sarah saw a flash of fear cross her brother's eyes. "It was his grandfather."

"Oh." Ben nodded and poured the marshmallow cereal into his bowl. "So, you'll have to take me and pick me up." He looked at her with uncertainty. "You don't know the rules for picking up and dropping off."

Sarah took a sip and grinned. "I don't think it takes a rocket scientist to figure out how to pull up in front of the school to pick you up."

"If you say so." He shoved a large spoonful of cereal and milk into his mouth. "What about lunch?" he asked around a mouthful of food. Milk dribbling down the corners of his mouth.

She grimaced, sat her cup down and reached for a napkin. "First," she swiped at his mouth, "don't talk with food in your mouth." She tossed the paper napkin in the trash. "Second, you usually buy your lunch."

"Yes, but they told me I have an overdue lunch debt, so I didn't get to get a regular tray yesterday."

She froze.

"They gave me the sandwich tray. It was soggy and smelled funny, so I didn't eat it." He shoveled more food into his mouth.

"Why didn't you tell me?" Now her brother was going hungry because she'd forgotten to pay the lunch bill.

He shrugged.

"And why didn't the school tell me you have a lunch debt? Don't they usually send a note home?" Sarah looked around for his backpack. She found it on the floor beside the refrigerator, picked it up, and unzipped it. She pulled out papers and quickly flipped through them.

Her fingers stopped when she came to his spelling test, which had a large red F on the top.

"Johnny. You made an F on your spelling test." Sarah squinted at the date. "This was three weeks ago, and it says I needed to sign it."

He shrugged. "I guess I forgot."

Sarah ran her hand through her long light brown ombre hair and sat down next to him. "Shouldn't I be getting a report card or something telling me how you're doing in school?" She narrowed her eyes.

"I guess."

"The last one I saw was at Christmas. It's almost spring break and you should get one pretty soon."

He ignored her and kept eating his sugary breakfast.

Sarah glanced at the time on the microwave, feeling the weight of the fact she was failing at this parenting thing … again. How could she expect a little kid to be the responsible one? Sarah sighed, knowing she needed to do better. Then again, she was already doing the best she knew how.

"Look, finish eating. I'll go get dressed and take you to school. We need to get this all straightened out." Sarah stood up and made her way into the bedroom. Opening her closet, she quickly found a cinnamon-colored Boho skirt. After slipping it on, she paired it with her cropped sleeveless linen top. Thankfully, it was now warm enough where she didn't have to wear sweaters any more.

She stepped into some jeweled sandals before heading into the bathroom to fix her hair and put on her makeup.

When she was done, she stepped back and looked at herself in the mirror. She was going to have to go in to talk to Johnny's teacher about his grades and why she wasn't getting any notes about his lunch debt. You'd think teachers would be on top of things like that.

Sarah sighed and pulled out her long gold necklace and slipped it over her head.

Did she look like the other moms at school?

No.

But then again, she wasn't a mom. She was the legal guardian of her brother who was doing the best she could.

It would have to be enough.

CHAPTER 3

Sarah pulled her van into an empty parking spot and killed the engine.

"You're going to get in trouble," her little brother warned.

"How?" She scowled at him.

"You can't park while the car line is going." He yawned and rubbed his eyes.

She gave him a look. "Well, that's just stupid."

"It's school. School rules are stupid." He shrugged. He made no motion to open the door.

"Aren't you going to get out?"

He glanced over his shoulder at the entrance of the school and then looked at her. "No. Mrs. Simpkins is walking over here to tell you to get back in the carline. Might as well stay buckled up."

"What?" She looked in the rearview mirror but didn't see anyone headed towards her.

Three sharp raps on her driver's side window made

her jump. She turned and saw a teacher in her fifties wearing a lanyard with the name Simpkins.

Mrs. Simpkins made a motion for Sarah to roll down her window.

Sarah reached for the hand crank and rolled the window down.

"Hi, I'm sorry but there is no parking during the carline." She looked past her to Johnny. "Johnny, that's going to put you being late for the first period."

Sarah shook her head. "I'm here because I need to talk to his teacher. It's important."

"Very well. But you'll have to wait until they finish the carline before you park. I can walk Johnny inside so he won't be late."

"Let me get this straight. I have to leave and then come back and park."

Mrs. Simpkins smiled. "Yes, once they finish the car line."

"What if I don't get out of my car but just sit here and then go inside once they finish the carline?"

"Sorry. That would be against the rules. Leave, then come back and park after they finish the carline."

"That's the stupidest rule I've ever heard." Sarah muttered to herself.

Johnny snickered.

"Excuse me?" The smile melted off Mrs. Simpkins' weathered face.

Sarah shook her head. "Nothing." She looked over at her brother. "Mrs. Simpkins will walk you in. Don't forget your backpack."

"Fine." After he opened the door and clamored out of the van, he slung his backpack on one shoulder.

Sarah made a mental note to remind him to wear his backpack properly or else he'd have back issues when he got older.

She forced a smile at Mrs. Simpkins, who put her hand on Johnny's shoulder while escorting him to the front door.

Sarah noticed the woman glanced back and glared at her, making sure she was indeed moving out of the parking spot.

Muttering several unflattering things about Mrs. Simpkins, Sarah put the van in reverse, heading out of the school parking lot.

She checked the time and realized she had fifteen minutes until the carline was officially over. She headed two blocks from the school to the local coffee shop, Heavenly Beans. Sarah pulled into the only empty parking spot available and killed the engine. She grabbed her leather fringe bag and slung it over her shoulder.

She got in line, glancing around for an empty seat as she waited her turn to order.

"Sarah?"

She turned at the sound of her name.

A wave of familiarity washed over her. She blinked at the man with blue eyes, wearing a suit and tie, standing behind her. "Noah? Noah Ellington?"

He smiled, flashing a set of white teeth against a dark black beard. "You remembered."

"Yeah, well, we went to school together. Although the beard almost threw me off. But the eyes are the same." She blinked, shocked to see Noah standing in front of her.

"Aren't you going to give me a hug?" He held out his arms.

"Are you sure? In a small town, they'll have us married by dinnertime." She laughed and hugged him.

"I doubt it," he said, pulling away. "Been there, done that." He smiled.

Her smiled slipped. She blinked. "Oh, I didn't know." She looked around to see if a female was waiting on him. "Is she here? I'd love to meet her."

Noah gave her a strained look. "I'm no longer married."

"Oh, sorry. I didn't know you divorced. My parents never kept up with my friends."

"Not divorced either."

She frowned.

"I'm a widower."

CHAPTER 4

*S*arah blinked. Noah? A widower? But he was so young.

"Ma'am. Can I take your order?" The barista spoke, shaking Sarah out of her shock at Noah's announcement.

"Sorry, yes. Can I get a large Caramel Macchiato with two shots of espresso?" She pulled out her debit card and handed it to the barista. She quickly rang her up and promptly presented her with the coffee. "Thank you."

"Do you have a minute? There's an empty table outside where we could sit and catch up." Noah smiled as the barista took his order next.

Sarah glanced at the clock on the wall. "Sure. I can't go back to the school until the car line is finished. I don't remember the school having stupid rules like that."

"Ah, I see you must have run into Mrs. Simpkins.

She runs the carline with an iron fist." Noah laughed, took his black coffee and led the way outside to the tables.

"So, you know her?" She looked at him before sitting in the black wrought-iron chair.

"Oh yes. Nathalie has her for English."

"Nathalie?" She took a sip of her coffee.

"My daughter." He took a sip of his coffee. "She's in Johnny's class."

"Really? I didn't know." She shifted in her seat.

"I haven't seen you at any of the field trips they've had."

She curled her hands around her coffee, feeling worse than she normally did about her parenting efforts.

"It's just that … well, after our parents died, I had a really hard time. Candy, Ben's mother, was kind enough to take Johnny to and from school. I told her I would carpool with her, but she said don't worry about it, that she had to volunteer at the school, anyway. So I just let her. As far as field trips, I offered to volunteer, but they already had reached their limits on parents." She shrugged, wondering why she felt the need to make excuses. She didn't owe anyone an explanation. Not really. She drew a deep breath and continued. "But now I have to go back to school and talk to Johnny's teacher. His grades are not good, so now I'm worried. I don't think I know what I'm doing with this parent thing," she admitted.

Noah reached over and squeezed her arm. "Welcome to the club. I'm trying to figure out how to dress Nathalie. And don't even ask me about fixing her hair. She wanted a French braid like Lilly, so I had to YouTube it." He scrubbed his hand over his face. "I got a call from the teacher asking if she had permission to redo her hair." He laughed. "I'm a total mess."

Sarah laughed, feeling the most relaxed she had in a while. "What's up with the suit and tie? I never thought you would go into an occupation that required a suit and tie. What do you do for a living?"

"I'm a financial planner." He smiled.

"Ah. You were always good with numbers. I believe you saved me from flunking algebra class," Sarah shuddered. "I think they should teach you stuff you're actually going to use. How did you decide on becoming a financial planner?"

Noah laughed. "I needed a secure job. And everyone needs a financial planner."

She shrugged. "Maybe. Maybe not."

He cocked his head. "You haven't changed a bit, Sarah. Still living life on your own terms, I see. The girl who was going to travel and conquer the world. I see you made good on your promise."

She laughed bitterly. "Conquer the world, not so much. It seems fate has other ideas for me. I didn't expect to be back in Hopeton."

"I'm sorry about your parents. I came to the funeral. But there were so many people coming up to you, and you looked exhausted, so I gave you some room."

Sarah rubbed her thumb along the seam of the

paper cup. "Thanks for that. That whole day seemed like a blur. I remembered it was raining." She couldn't remember if the myth about raining during a funeral was a good omen or bad.

Silence stretched between them.

Noah cleared his throat. "Are you letting Johnny go to the cub scout campout this weekend?"

She frowned. "I knew nothing about it. Was there a sign-up sheet or something?"

"Actually, he got it at the last cub scout meeting. Candy should have given you the sheet." Noah took a sip of his coffee.

Sarah sighed. "Johnny said nothing about it. I'm not sure he'll want to go without Ben."

Noah nodded. "Those two are inseparable. It's good he's got a best friend like Ben. But I think Johnny will regret it if he doesn't go. Other dads have volunteered to go as well. You can come too."

She arched her eyebrow. "Will they let me in? I thought it was a guy thing."

Noah laughed. "Before I became the cub scout leader, Laura Hudson was the leader. She's Jeffrey's mom. It's hard to find volunteers to help. It seems everyone is so busy with their jobs, and life, and ... "

"Mental breakdowns." She sipped. "Tell me about how you are managing the single parent stuff. I welcome any advice. I feel like I'm constantly failing at everything."

He sighed. "I think we all feel that way. Nathalie

was very young when Lucy, her mom, died. She doesn't remember much about her."

"How did you two meet? I don't remember going to school with a girl named Lucy."

"I met her during senior year. She didn't go to our school. There was a chess tournament that involved all the surrounding schools. She ended up beating me. We started dating. Then Lucy got pregnant on graduation night. Definitely not what we had planned."

"I'm sure." Sarah found his total honesty refreshing. "Were you nervous when you found out?'"

"Nervous? No. Freaked out. Yes. I thought my life was over and I was going to be bagging groceries for the rest of my life."

"Can't buy diapers on that kind of budget." She grinned.

"No doubt. We got married before Nathalie was born, and I kept on with my plans of college."

Sarah took another sip of her coffee. "Can I ask?"

"You are wondering how Lucy died?" Noah nodded. "Nathalie was a toddler, and it was summertime. I was taking extra summer classes to graduate early. Lucy left Nathalie in the crib and went to the mailbox to get the mail. A bee stung her. She was allergic and apparently didn't know it. She made it to the steps of our house before she went into anaphylactic shock and died. When our neighbor found her, he called 911."

"Oh my gosh, Noah," she reached for her arm. "I'm so sorry. You must have felt like a train had hit you."

He nodded. "You have no idea. It was so surreal. Something so simple could be so deadly."

"Does Nathalie have any allergies?"

"No. I had her checked for every possible allergic reaction there is."

She cocked her head. "When you go camping with the cub scouts, do you bring your daughter?"

"No. She usually stays with her grandparents." Noah said, his face revealing how disappointed that made him.

She sent him a commiserating smile. "She's missing out by not camping. The best sunsets I've ever seen are out in the middle of nature, away from everyone. There was one particular sunset in the dessert in Utah during the spring." She smiled as she recalled the memory.

"Sounds beautiful." He paused, then a slow grin broke out across his face. "You should come this weekend. We are camping at the state park an hour from here. You should drive your van. I bet the boys would get a kick out of seeing it. Might make them want to take on a project like that when they get out of high school."

"I'll think about it." She glanced at the clock on the wall. "I have to be going. I've got to meet with Johnny's teacher about his grades." She gathered up her purse and nearly empty coffee cup and stood.

As Noah stood, he straightened his tie. "It was good to see you. And think about camping out this weekend. It would be good for both of you."

Sarah studied Noah. "I'll definitely think about it. Thanks for the chat."

"Any time." He smiled.

Sarah walked toward her van, her heart somehow a little lighter.

CHAPTER 5

*B*y the time Sarah arrived back at school, the car line was gone. Breathing a sigh of relief, she pulled into the parking spot in front of the school and got out.

She slid her sunglasses over her eyes and headed for the front door. Once inside, the hallway was empty except for a boy dragging his backpack down the hall towards a classroom.

When Sarah spotted the office, which was basically a wall of glass, she walked inside. A lone kid sitting in a worn chair swinging his legs back and forth glanced up at her and then went back to studying the floor. The only adult she saw was the secretary, wearing reading glasses on a silver chain and typing away on the computer.

"Can I help you?" The secretary snapped as she looked up, but didn't stop typing. She was in her late sixties, thin cruel lips that seemed to disapprove of everything modern, and a distinct mole on her chin, sprouting a brown hair.

"Hello. I need to see Mrs. Wallace." Sarah forced herself not to look at the woman's mole.

"She's in class right now. Do you have an appointment?" The woman continued to type away as she narrowed her eyes.

Sarah pushed her annoyance down and drew a deep breath. "No. I don't. This is important. I need to talk to her about Johnny Williams' grades," she explained, talking slowly and with purpose.

The woman finally stopped typing and turned her attention to Sarah. "And you are?"

"His legal guardian." Trying to get an appointment to see a teacher was like trying to get into Fort Knox.

Very different from when she went to school.

"I see." The woman picked up the phone and punched in some numbers. She spoke in a low voice that Sarah couldn't hear.

The lady across from her put the phone back down. "Mrs. Wallace said she will meet with you, but you'll have to schedule a time."

Frustrated, Sarah shoved her glasses in her purse. "Fine. How do I go about making an appointment? Or do I need to draw a lottery ticket and hope I get to speak to someone?"

The woman behind the desk narrowed her eyes and opened her mouth. Before she could speak, the door to the office opened and a woman wearing a black pantsuit came bustling in.

"Carol, open my office door for me before I drop all these files."

"Yes, Principal Wheeler." Carol hopped up from her desk and quickly opened the door to the office. The principal stepped inside.

Sarah narrowed her eyes. "Principal Wheeler?" She stopped at the office door and peered inside.

"Yes, can I help you?" The principal plopped her files down on the desk, looking up at Sarah.

"Yes, I'm Sarah..."

"You're Sarah Williams. I know who you are." The principal stood and straightened her shoulders.

"Yes, well, I'm trying to speak to Johnny's teacher, but apparently, I have to make an appointment. I'm afraid that this is quite urgent. It's about his grades."

"Like I told her, she has to make an appointment." Carol crossed her arms and shot Sarah a glare.

Sarah glared back. She'd been on her own long enough not to let other people intimidate her.

"It's okay, Carol. I'll talk to Miss Williams."

A sour look crossed Carol's face as she stepped out of the room and closed the door behind her.

"Please sit."

Sarah sat in the leather chair across from Principal Wheeler.

"What can I do for you?" Principal wheeler clasped her hands on the desk.

"I'm concerned about Johnny's grades. I went through his backpack and found a spelling test with an F. And it wasn't recent. I thought his grades were okay, considering … everything. But when I found the F, I grew very concerned."

Principal Wheeler nodded her head. "That is concerning," she acknowledged. "Let me pull up his grades on the computer and see if Mrs. Wallace has left any comments."

Principal Wheeler turned on her computer and waited a few seconds before typing on the keyboard.

Carol opened the door and sat a large Styrofoam cup of coffee in front of Principal Wheeler.

"Thanks, Carol."

"You're welcome." Carol narrowed her eyes at Sarah. Sarah couldn't help but look at the woman's mole.

"Ellison Whitmore is waiting for you. His teacher sent him in before the school bell rang. He was bullying little Nathalie again."

Principal Wheeler sighed and nodded. "I'll see him as soon as I'm done here."

"And there's a call from a parent on hold. Didn't say what they wanted." Again, Carol sent Sarah a glare.

Sarah gave Carol a brilliant smile in order to kill the woman with kindness.

Carol looked away, clearly irritated by Sarah's presence.

"Take a message." Principal Wheeler went back to typing, effectively excusing Carol.

"Yes, ma'am." Carol closed the door behind her.

Sarah clasped her hands in her lap as she watched Principal Wheeler's demeanor stiffen.

"I see." She stopped typing and sat back in her chair. "Mrs. Wallace has sent numerous notes home with Johnny to discuss his slipping grades. When she didn't get a reply, she sent emails."

Sarah frowned and pulled out her phone. "Emails? I don't remember getting any emails."

She pulled up her email and quickly checked the new messages. "I see nothing. And I even looked in my spam box."

Principal Wheeler frowned. "Hmm. Let me see where she sent the emails." She typed some more and then stopped. "Oh, I see. It seems she's been sending them to what looks like your mother's email."

Sarah grimaced. "Well, no wonder. I don't even have access to that account. Why would she even send an email … " She wanted to say a dead woman, but the words wouldn't come out.

"It is the only email we have on file for him. She probably thought you had access to that email. Not to mention, Mrs. Wallace has a lot on her plate with all the kids in her class. What's your email and I'll add it?" Principal Wheeler waited for her to answer.

Sarah repeated her email address and lifted her chin. "I always check his backpack after dinner. I don't know why I didn't see any notes from Mrs. Wallace. Maybe they're getting lost."

There was a knock on the door, and then the security guard poked his head in.

"I'm in a meeting." She scowled.

"I know, and I apologize. But the boys' bathroom is flooding. Again."

Principal Wheeler blew out a breath. "Have the janitor mop it up and block it off to keep the kids out. Then tell Carol to call a plumber. Again."

"Will do." The security guard darted out.

Principal Wheeler turned her attention back to her. "Sorry about that. I'm pulled in a thousand directions it seems." She took a sip of her coffee and looked at her. "Maybe the notes are getting … misplaced."

Both of them knew the notes weren't getting lost. Johnny had been hiding them from her.

"I know it's been hard for you and your brother since your parents' death." Principal Wheeler gave her a sympathetic look. "It was a shock to the whole town when we heard."

Sara nodded. "This was the last place I thought I'd be. Back in Hopeton and raising my little brother." She swallowed back the emotion rising in her throat. "I need to know what to do to get his grades up. Is it all classes he is failing or just spelling? Is there a chance they will hold him back a year?" Worry gnawed at her stomach.

Principal Wheeler looked at the computer and then back at her.

"His lowest grade is spelling and reading. That's not surprising. If a child has a low grade in one, then he'll have a low grade in the other. His math and science grades are average, but I know he can do better."

Sarah nodded. "Is there a tutor I can hire? Or some extra things he can do to bring up his grade?"

Principal Wheeler studied her computer screen. "It looks like he is late on turning in several book reports. I'll speak with Mrs. Wallace to see if she would accept them if he turns them in, even though they are late. That means he has a lot of reading to do. He'll have to give up some things like playing with his friends after school and video games."

"And the cub scout camping trip this weekend." Sarah muttered.

"Actually, I wouldn't cancel that. It's important for Johnny to stay involved with his cub scouts. And he can take his book with him to read before bed. Will you be accompanying him to the camp out?" Principal Wheeler clasped her hands under her chin and studied her.

As much as she wanted to say no, she figured she needed to do all she could to get in Principal Wheeler's good graces.

"I talked to Noah Ellington this morning about it." Sarah nodded.

"Good. Noah is a great cub scout leader. He also understands your situation and that will help Johnny." Principal Wheeler smiled. "Since you are doing your part to help Johnny, I'll go in and watch Mrs. Wallace's class while she comes and talks to you in here. That way, you don't have to make an appointment."

Sarah's eyes widened. "Thank you. I appreciate it."

Principal Wheeler stood with her coffee cup. The

dark brown liquid sloshed on her shirt. "No trouble. Sometimes, schools make stupid rules. Unfortunately, I don't have the power to undo them." She headed for the door, wiping her shirt with a paper napkin.

Sarah was liking Principal Wheeler with each passing minute.

CHAPTER 6

*A*fter a few brief minutes, a pretty woman with dark hair and dark eyes walked into the principal's office. She wore tan slacks and a pink button-down shirt with sensible shoes. She looked to be in her thirties.

"You must be Johnny's sister. I'm Mrs. Wallace." She held out her hand and smiled.

"I'm Sarah Williams." Sarah shook hands and then Mrs. Wallace sat in the principal's chair.

"I'm sorry that I didn't make an appointment. I'm still trying to figure out the rules."

"That's okay. You two have been through a lot. I'm glad you came to see me. Principal Wheeler updated me on what you two talked about. I will accept his book reports, but he has to get them done within three weeks."

Sarah gave her a grateful smile. "Thank you."

"And I'm sorry you haven't been getting my emails.

The only email address I had on file was your mom's and, of course, her brother, Oliver, since she had him listed as an emergency contact. I copied him on everything I sent, so I'm sure he's caught you up."

Sarah's stomach dropped. "Wait. Uncle Oliver?"

"Yes." Mrs. Wallace frowned. "I met him at the funeral and he explained that he would help a great deal with Johnny. He said you were too young to be caring for a child that young."

Sarah felt like someone had hit her with a baseball bat. She'd not talked to Uncle Oliver since the funeral. Not that she minded. She was never close to him when she was a child, and he only came around when it was convenient to him or when he needed a place to stay. When she tried to warn her mother that he was a user, she always brushed Sarah off and said he was a free spirit. She even suggested that he had a lot in common with Sarah, which really infuriated her.

Sarah thoroughly disagreed. In fact, she believed there was something very sinister about Uncle Oliver. While she couldn't put her finger on the exact thing that made her feel so cautious, everything inside her warned there was something subtle that could turn dangerous if one wasn't on their toes.

Sarah bit back a response and masked her concern with a pasted smile. "I'm afraid that Uncle Oliver is not the legal guardian of Johnny. He spoke out of turn. I'm the legal guardian of my brother. I gave my email to Principal Wheeler. I have to insist that from now on you only contact me."

31

Mrs. Wallace sent her a pained look. "Of course. Miss Williams, I'm so sorry if I caused any issues between you and your uncle. It wasn't my intent. And he seemed so sincere."

"It's not your fault at all. No need to apologize." Sarah smiled and thought it best to change the subject. "I was telling Principal Wheeler about the Cub Scout camp-out this weekend. I was thinking Johnny needed to stay home to study, but she said to let him go."

Mrs. Wallace brightened. "Yes, I agree. Let him go and he can take his book with him. Will you be going as a chaperone?"

"I think I may need to. So he can be sure to read his book at night."

"Great idea. Reading around a campfire sure brings back memories for me as a child. And Johnny needs to interact more with his friends. Since his…your parents' death, he seems to be a little more hesitant to join in with the other kids. I'm sure it's something he's working through, but I just wanted to let you know."

"Thank you, I really appreciate that. I should let you get back to class." As Sarah stood, she held out her hand.

Mrs. Wallace took it and smiled. "And in case you haven't been told, you're doing a great job taking care of Johnny."

As she drove back home, Sarah let those words play over and over in her head.

She needed to hear it, but she wasn't so sure they were true.

CHAPTER 7

*A*fter her meeting at school, Sarah headed home to get a jump on the day. She walked through the front door to the coconut scent of her favorite candle, White Beaches, and suppressed a yawn. She'd stayed up late last night working on a new song she was writing, because she'd been so caught up in the lyrics, she had forgotten about the time. Now her late night was catching up with her.

Sarah headed into the kitchen and started the kettle to make a cup of tea. Once the kettle whistled, she turned off the stove. She plopped an English breakfast tea bag into a mug and poured the water over it. She set the timer on her phone and then looked out the kitchen window at the lake, waiting for her tea to steep.

She loved growing up on the lake. They had summer filled days of swimming and water skiing, while winters were all about building snowmen and sledding.

The timer on her phone buzzed, bringing her out of her emotional trip down memory lane. She disposed of the tea bag in the garbage and took a sip.

There was a lot to do today before she picked up Johnny. First, she had to get caught up on laundry. With only two of them, how did they have so many dirty clothes? Sighing, she took her cup of tea and her overflowing basket of laundry and headed for the washing machine.

When she finally finished with laundry and picking up the house, it was almost two o'clock.

Sarah flung herself on the couch as she sighed, determined not to shut her eyes for a second. She couldn't be late for the carline. Who knew what penalties that would cause?

The doorbell rang, jolting her out of her relaxed stupor.

She forced her feet to the floor and made her way to the front door.

Opening the door, it shocked her to see Hannah Reece standing there.

"Ms. Hannah. I wasn't expecting you." She frowned.

"Sorry to drop in on you, but I wanted to catch you before Johnny got home from school." Hannah smiled. "Instead of bringing you a casserole tonight, I'd like to invite you and Johnny to come eat dinner at my house. Carolina will be there as well."

Sarah blinked. "That's very generous of you. Good

manners dictate I should decline and then have you invite me again, but to be honest, I'm just exhausted. I think Johnny is tired of frozen pizza, too. Dinner would be lovely. Thank you."

"You're very welcome. How did the chicken work out last Friday night?" Hannah cocked her head.

Sarah shook her head. "*Your* chicken dish was wonderful. But when I tried to remake it from the recipe card you included, I failed miserably. I seem to get distracted and burn something. I think I'm just destined to survive on chicken nuggets and macaroni and cheese."

Hannah threw her head back and laughed. "I doubt that. Cooking takes time and you can't rush yourself. Most of all, don't give up. The first month I tried making homemade biscuits was awful. They came out hard as a baseball and I threw them out to the birds, but even the blackbirds didn't dare touch them. Finally, I threw them in the lake where they promptly sank."

Sarah laughed.

"Just don't give up. You'll get there." Hannah glanced over her shoulder. "I've got to run to the store to grab a few ingredients. I'll see you both around six thirty. And tell Johnny that Carolina is bringing Phoenix." Hannah waved before getting into her Mercedes.

Sarah waved back and shut the door. "At least I don't have to cook tonight," she muttered to herself. She glanced at the time on her phone. Time to pick up Johnny from school.

Grabbing her keys, she got into her van.

Hopefully she'd get to the school early enough to be first in line. That way, they could go straight home to work on homework and reading until time to head over to Hannah's for dinner.

Like everything else in her life, her plans didn't go as she wanted.

She didn't know she couldn't get in the car line until exactly ten minutes till three. Sarah had pulled to the front door at fifteen minutes till three and the security guard made her leave. Getting in her van, she circled the block and by the time she got back, she was in the back of the line.

She got home around four o'clock and gave Johnny a snack of store-bought cookies and milk, which he complained about, saying they didn't taste like Hannah's homemade cookies.

When they sat down to work on homework, it was like pulling teeth to get him to stop getting distracted and get some work done. He was so distracted. But with the promise of dinner at Hannah's, Sarah convinced Johnny to try.

They worked on homework and reading until dinner time.

"Go brush your hair and wash your hands. We don't want to be late." Sarah called upstairs to her brother.

She heard him mutter but was too tired to ask what he was griping about now. Instead, she slipped on a denim jacket over her skirt and crop top and added a camel-colored hat to the ensemble.

Johnny ran downstairs and raced out the door. "Let's go. I'm starving."

She gritted her teeth as she shut the door behind her and locked it. Johnny was waiting at the van, but she shook her head. "No. Let's walk. The weather is too nice and we both need to stretch our legs."

He pulled a face but didn't argue. Instead, he headed down the driveway.

Sarah quickly caught up to him. "After dinner, we'll get started on your reading assignment. Which book did you want to read first? Diary of a Wimpy Kid or Because of Winn Dixie?"

"They both sound stupid. Plus, I saw the Diary of a Wimpy Kid movie."

She cut her eyes at him. "The movie always has some differences from the book."

He said nothing as he continued walking toward Hannah's house, his hands stuffed in his jeans' pocket.

"How was school today? Anything interesting happen?"

"Paul got sent to the office again. And I didn't have anyone to sit next to at lunch. Not that it mattered. Since they gave me the nasty sandwich tray again because I'm overdue for my lunch money."

Sarah stopped in her tracks and gasped. "Johnny. I totally forgot! I'm so sorry I forgot to pay." She didn't think she could feel any worse about her day, but she was wrong.

"I'll make it up to you tomorrow. I'll get online and

pay your lunch debt and if you want, I'll make you an extra special lunch to take with you."

"You?" His eyes widened.

"Yeah. Don't you think I'm getting better with Hannah's help? I mean, you liked the dishes she's been bringing over."

"I do like Ms. Hannah's food. But your meals don't taste anything like hers." He turned up the driveway leading to Hannah's house.

She frowned. "Yeah, that chicken dish didn't go as planned. I'll just do better next time."

"Right," Johnny sighed with disappointment, and then ran up the driveway to the front door. He pushed the doorbell three times before Sarah could catch up to him.

The door swung open, and Hannah stood there with a smile. "Johnny, hello! I hope you're ready for a home cooked meal."

"I'm half starved to death." He stepped inside.

Sarah gritted her teeth and followed him inside.

CHAPTER 8

"*T*hat meatloaf was really good. And the potatoes and vegetables were amazing." Sarah placed her napkin beside her plate and looked at Hannah.

"Yes, Hannah, this meal was wonderful," Carolina smiled at her friend across the table.

"Thank you for having us. After the day I've had, eating a hot meal that someone else prepared has been a treat." Sarah admitted. "It certainly beats chicken nuggets and macaroni and cheese."

"I'm so glad you enjoyed it," Hannah smiled. "And there's enough for you to take some leftovers home."

"Yay!" Johnny swiped his face with the back of his hand. "Can I take them for lunch tomorrow? So I don't starve?" He looked at Sarah.

She ignored his barb and frowned. "Will they let you use the microwave at school?"

"Yes, it's by the table where the teachers sit."

"Sure. You can have it for lunch." Sarah smiled.

Phoenix let out a whine.

"He needs to go out," Carolina stood up, but Johnny slid out of his chair first.

"I'll take him. I'm trying to teach him how to fetch." Johnny ran over to the back door and patted his hands on his legs. "Come on, Phoenix. Come on, boy."

The three women watched as Phoenix raced out the back door as soon as Johnny opened it. The boy laughed and chased after the dog.

"If he can get him to fetch, that will be some trick. The vet told me that Phoenix was around eight years old. And you know what they say, can't teach an old dog new tricks." Carolina chortled.

"I bet that dog can learn to do anything, including fetch. Remember that time he rang my doorbell with his nose?" Hannah grinned.

"He did? When was this?" Sarah looked at the women.

"It happened around Christmas. I remember because there was snow on the ground." Carolina nodded. "He's pretty smart for a stray. I bet he belonged to someone before he adopted me."

Sarah had heard the story about how Phoenix had just showed up at Carolina's lake house. After searching for his owners, and not finding them, Carolina kept the dog and named him Phoenix. Like her, he was starting over again and rising from the ashes.

Hannah held up the bottle of Josh Pinot Grigio. "Anyone need a refill?"

"I'll take a small refill. We still have reading to do when we get home," Sarah held her glass out while Hannah poured the wine. "I didn't think Johnny could resent me more, but after I told him he couldn't play any more video games until his grades came up, he had a fit."

"How are things going?" Carolina cocked her head. "I'm sure it's hard to balance everything you've got going on and raising your brother."

Sarah took a sip. "It's certainly not a place I expected to be at twenty-six. This time last year I was camping out in Leads, Colorado and singing at a bar for tips. But here I am, back in Hopeton with a brother who hates me and thinks I can't do anything right."

"Johnny doesn't hate you. He is still grieving his parents, and probably feels robbed of his normal life."

"So do I." Sarah mumbled before taking a sip.

Carolina folded her hands under her chin and sighed. "I am so fascinated by your life, Sarah."

Sarah cringed. "Me?"

"Yes, you. I mean, you're young, beautiful, a singer, and I heard through the grapevine that you are also a songwriter."

Hannah snorted. "The grapevine is Bernice, isn't it?"

Carolina frowned. "How'd you know?"

"Because she knows everything about everybody." Hannah shook her head. "But yes, Sarah has an amazing voice." She looked back at Sarah. "I remember the first time you sang in church."

"You do?" Sarah blinked. That seemed like a million years ago.

"Yes. Milly Hamilton was supposed to sing a Christmas special. She got up to the microphone and froze when she saw all the people in the audience." Hannah tapped her finger to her chin. "I believe it was O Holy Night."

"What happened?" Carolina leaned forward.

"When Milly froze, everyone kept waiting. Finally, Sarah steps forward, takes the microphone off the stand and starts singing like she's done it all her life." A smile blossomed on Hannah's face. "She received a standing ovation."

Sarah frowned. "I did? I don't remember that. All I remember is Milly standing there like a turkey, not moving or singing. It was past dinner, and I had missed lunch. I was hungry. My parents told me that after the Christmas special was over, we could go get something to eat. O Holy Night was the last song to be performed. I was starving." Sarah shook her head. "I guess I was more motivated by eating than anything."

Hannah laughed and took a sip of her wine.

Sarah sighed. "You know, when I was out traveling, I was always prepared to sing. No matter the setting or the circumstance. Like the time, the lights went out in the bar where I was singing. There was confusion at first with the band, but I grabbed my guitar and kept singing. Or the time someone stole my wallet and couldn't pay for my dinner. I asked the manager if I could sing for him that night to pay for it. I actually made enough money to pay for my meal and have gas money to get me to the next town. But with raising a kid, I don't feel prepared at all. It's like one roadblock after another."

Hannah reached over and squeezed her hand. "That's parenting, honey."

"Hannah says you have a van that you converted all by yourself. I'd love to look at it sometimes." Carolina's eyes sparkled.

"I didn't bring my van. We walked over here. Otherwise I would step outside and show it to you. But you are certainly welcome to stop by anytime, and I'll show it to you." She smiled at Carolina. Sarah liked her immediately. Carolina was around the age of a lot of the mothers who had children in elementary school, yet she never made Sarah feel bad for wearing crop tops or not dressing like the other moms. She never got a haughty look from Carolina like the looks she got from the other moms at school.

"Were you ever scared of going across the country by yourself?" Hannah took a sip of wine.

"Scared? Not really. If I camped somewhere I didn't feel safe, then I gave myself permission to leave, even if it was in the middle of the night. That only happened twice. But I got lonely. I remember this one time, I had driven all day and finally camped at this secluded spot in Missouri. There was this small river and a waterfall at the end. The way the sun had set on the water was breathtaking. I slept out under the stars that night. And this sense of loneliness washed over me so strongly that I started crying. I fell asleep crying. When I woke up, the sun was rising, the birds were singing, and the feeling of loneliness had disappeared. For me, it was nature's way of telling me I was never alone."

"That's beautiful." Hannah cocked her head. "If your songs are as beautiful as that, I bet you're going to be a star one day."

Sarah snorted. "I'm afraid my dreams of making it big will not happen. I can't take off at a moment's notice to sing at a venue."

"I wouldn't be so sure. You know God has a way of putting a dream in your heart for a reason." Hannah whispered.

"Maybe He should put some more money in my bank account if He's doling out favors." Sarah took a sip of her wine.

Carolina leaned forward. "Are you in a financial bind?"

Sarah went wide-eyed, wishing she hadn't slipped up, and mentioned the fact that she struggled to make ends meet.

"I'm so sorry, Sarah, I didn't mean to offend you," Carolina cringed. "Or be nosy. I've been in a situation where I found myself … starting over from scratch. I had no professional career and work experience. After my husband of twenty years divorced me for a girl half his age, I found myself alone. If there's anything I can do, please ask."

"Just so you know, your ex-husband is a fool." Sarah grinned.

"Thanks. I think so, too." Carolina nodded.

Sarah relaxed and nodded. Her gaze flickered out to the backyard where Phoenix and Johnny were running around playing keep away with a stick.

"It's okay. I don't really have anyone I can talk about my situation to." Sarah gave Carolina a grateful smile. "When our parents died, they left Johnny a substantial inheritance. It's split up so he will get it when he is eighteen, twenty-one and twenty-eight. They left me some money as well, but not nearly as much. In the will, they stated I had always shown an independence that assured them I could always take care of myself. I haven't touched the money they left me. I'm going to use it to move to Los Angeles and maybe get a record deal, after Johnny graduates, of course. As far as bills, the house is paid off, so I just maintain the utilities and food with money I've saved from singing at restaurants and bars when I was traveling. I can't do that now, so, in the meantime, I need to figure out how to find a job."

Carolina nodded and smiled. "I believe you told me you volunteered at animal shelters while you traveled? Have you checked with them? Maybe they are hiring?"

Sarah sighed. "I already called the two in Hopeton and they don't have any hiring positions. There are not a lot of jobs for people with no degree or work experience."

"What about Green Thumb Nursery?" Hannah

looked at Carolina. "Do you think Bernice would hire someone else?"

Carolina sighed. "I'm afraid not. I asked her about hiring someone for the spring. She shot me down. She said I was trying to cut into her profits by hiring more people."

"Let me ask around and see what I can come up with." Hannah frowned, lost in thought. "I'm sure there are jobs that would fit you."

"It has to be flexible hours where I can take Johnny to school and pick him up. So no night shifts." Sarah glanced at the time on her phone. "Wow, I didn't realize it was getting late. We should head home. Dinner was wonderful. Thank you so much. I really had a good time tonight." Sarah stood.

"I'm so glad." Hannah got to her feet. "I'm going to put these leftovers in a microwavable container for Johnny tomorrow."

"Thank you." Sarah smiled. "I really appreciate it. Now, if I can just get as good at cooking as you, we might actually have a chance at surviving and not starving to death."

CHAPTER 9

*T*he next morning, Sarah woke up to the sunlight streaming in through her bedroom. It was unusually quiet in the house.

Unease snaked in her stomach. Something was wrong.

She glanced at the clock on her nightstand. It was blank.

Blinking, she reached over and turned on the lamp. Nothing.

"Oh, no." She grabbed her phone. She was at three percent battery. She looked at the time on the screen.

Nine o'clock.

"Oh, sh..." She clamped her mouth shut and scrambled out of bed. She raced to Johnny's room and shook him awake.

"You've got to get up. We overslept." She hurried to the window and threw open the curtains to let the light spill into the room.

"What?" Johnny sat up, rubbing his eyes.

"The electricity is off and my alarm didn't ring. You've got to hurry. Get dressed!" She ran to his closet. She pulled out some jeans, a shirt and tossed them on his bed.

"Can't I just stay home?" he groused, stretching his arms over his head.

"No. Now hurry." Sarah ran out of his bedroom and into her room. She pulled out some denim shorts and a graphic T-shirt and quickly dressed. She slipped her feet into some white sneakers when she caught a glance of her reflection in the mirror. There wasn't time to do anything with her hair, so she grabbed a floral scarf and wrapped it around her head in a bandana style, letting the ends fall down past her shoulders.

"Let's go!" Sarah called out as she headed down the stairs. She stopped in the kitchen long enough to grab a strawberry Pop tart and filled a cup of milk.

"What about breakfast?" Johnny appeared at the door with a smudge of toothpaste on the corner of his mouth.

"Here." She shoved the Pop tart and the milk into his hands. She wiped the smear of toothpaste from his mouth with her finger.

He scowled. "Don't forget my lunch."

"Right." She washed her hands and grabbed the plastic container of food that Hannah had been kind enough to give her and put it in his backpack. She glanced around. "Am I forgetting something?"

He rolled his eyes at her. "My money for my lunch

debt."

Sarah grimaced. "Right." She dug around in her purse and pulled out a couple of twenties. "Will they let you pay Mrs. Wallace when you get to school?"

"No. I have to go to the office and pay Miss Carol." He shoved some Pop tart in his mouth.

"Never mind. I'll go inside and explain to everyone why you are late, and then I'll pay while I'm in there." She grabbed her keys and opened the door. "Let's get a move on, Johnny."

Sarah backed out of the driveway onto the main road. She glanced over at Hannah's house as they drove past. "That's weird. Her lights are on."

She looked at Carolina's house and noticed lights were on as well.

"Maybe it's just our house that the lights are off." She muttered.

"Maybe they turned off the electricity because you didn't pay the light bill." Johnny spoke around a mouthful of Pop tart.

"Why would you say that?" She glared.

"Because Lonnie got his electricity cut off when his dad forgot to pay the light bill. He said it was during the winter when his dad got fired. They had to go stay with his grandma for a week until they got the lights turned back on. Lonnie hates going to his grandma's house because she has a hundred cats."

She turned onto the road into town. "I'm sure Lonnie is exaggerating. His grandma doesn't have a hundred cats."

Johnny shook his head. "Lonnie doesn't exaggerate. That week he stayed at his grandma's, he came to school smelling like cat pee."

Sarah's mind raced. Come to think of it, she couldn't remember getting an electric bill in a few months. It must be some kind of mistake.

"After I drop you off, I'll go to the electric company and find out what the deal is."

A few short minutes later, she was pulling into an empty parking spot at school. They both got out of the van and hurried to the front door.

She spotted Carol, the secretary, glaring at her from the glassed-in office. "Ugh. She's gonna give me he ... heck." Sarah cut her eyes at her little brother, hoping he hadn't caught what she really wanted to say.

"Ms. Carol scares me." Johnny looked up at her. "She looks like Roz from Monsters Inc. Lonnie says her wart has an antenna coming out of it. And that she's an alien."

Sarah broke out into laughter. But when she saw how serious Johnny was, she contained herself.

"I'm sure she's not an alien. Just a very unhappy person."

"An unhappy person with an antenna coming out of her chin," Johnny added as she put her hand on his shoulder to hurry him up.

"Ms. Williams. I see Johnny is late," Carol sneered. "Johnny will get detention unless there's a valid reason for his tardiness."

"They cut off our electricity," Johnny blurted out.

Sarah wanted the floor to open up and swallow her.

A smirk played at the corners of Carol's cruel mouth. "Is that so?"

"That's not true. Our electricity was out this morning and my alarm didn't go off. Also, I need to pay for Johnny's lunch debt."

"Very well," Carol lifted her chin. "Johnny, you run along to your class."

Without so much as a goodbye, Johnny shot out of the office down the hallway to his class.

Carol typed something into her computer and then looked up at Sarah. "Johnny owes fifty dollars on his lunch debt."

"Fifty dollars?" She gaped.

"Yes. You have not paid his bill in months." Carol smirked. "Probably like your electric bill," she muttered, but Sarah heard the words perfectly clear.

Biting back a reply, Sarah slapped down the last hundred-dollar bill she had in her purse on the counter. "Here you go. Do I need to do anything else? Sign something? Say a vow? Give a pint of blood?"

"No. That's all." Carol dismissed her and went back to typing.

Sarah clenched her hands together and turned to leave when she almost ran into a little girl.

"Oh. I'm sorry. I didn't see you there," she offered the blonde-hair child a smile.

The girl looked up from the floor and a pair of very familiar blue eyes looked back at her.

51

"Nathalie, what do you need?" Carol looked over at the child.

Nathalie. This must be Noah's little girl. Sarah recognized the eyes right away.

"Mrs. Wallace asked me to come in here and wait for my dad to come pick me up."

"Okay, well ,just sit there and be quiet." Carol went back to her work on the computer.

Sarah knew she needed to get to the electric company to get her lights turned back on before picking up Johnny, but somehow, she couldn't take her eyes off Nathalie.

Sarah knelt in front of the little girl. "Hi, Nathalie. I'm Sarah. I'm a friend of your dad. In fact, we went to school together."

Nathalie looked at her under her long eyelashes.

"Are you sick? Is that why your dad is picking you up?"

Just then, Principal Wheeler's door flew open, and she stuck her head out. "Carol, can you come in here and tell me what I've done to my computer? The screen just went blank. Again."

"Certainly." Carol shot a warning glance at Sarah before getting up from her chair and heading into the office.

Sarah slowly stood. "Well, it was nice meeting you, Nathalie."

"My dad is picking me up because a boy in the class made fun of my hair. Then he stuck gum in it. Mrs. Wallace cut it out, but now she says my dad might have to take me to get my hair cut shorter because it's uneven."

"Can I see?" Sarah knelt back down and looked at the girl's head. There was a sizable gap where the gum had been cut out.

Nathalie blinked back tears.

"You know what, short hair is in fashion." Sarah smiled.

"I like long hair. I wish I had long hair like you." She reached out and touched a lock of Sarah's hair.

Sarah heard the door open, and she turned to see Noah standing there looking from her to Nathalie.

"Hi, Noah." She smiled. "I was just meeting Nathalie."

"Hi, Sarah" he said softly.

Sarah turned back to Nathalie. "I tell you what, why don't you take this and wear it until you get to the hair salon?"

"Can I?" A smile grew on Nathalie's face.

"Sure. I have loads of them." She unwrapped the scarf she'd tied as a bandana and began tying it around the child's head. She fiddled with it until she got it like she wanted and then stood. "Looks pretty good."

Nathalie looked at Noah for reassurance.

"It looks good." Noah walked over and knelt beside her. "Who knows, the stylist might fix it without cutting much length off."

"Can I keep the scarf?" Nathalie asked with wide-eyes.

"Nathalie," Noah scolded.

"Sure. Like I said, I have loads." Sarah hiked her purse up on her shoulder and looked at Noah. "So what happened to the kid that did this?"

Noah's eyes darkened. "His parents had to come pick him up, and he's suspended for three days."

"Nathalie, next time he does that, you stick gum in his hair." Sarah lifted her chin.

"Sarah, don't tell her that." Noah said under his breath. Thankfully, Nathalie was too busy admiring herself in the reflection of the glass to pay any attention to their conversation.

"She has to just sit there and take it?" Sarah narrowed her eyes.

Noah ran his hand through his hair and sighed. "Honestly, I don't know. It's all I can do not to throttle that boy."

"I can do it for you."

His lips curled into a grin. "Thanks. I'll keep it in mind. What are you doing here?"

"Late for school. Her electricity got cut off," Carol reported with a smirk as she came out of the principal's office.

"We were late for school, and I had to pay Johnny's lunch debt." She shot Carol a glare. "I need to be on my way."

"Bye, Sarah." Nathalie waved.

"By Nathalie." Sarah smiled at the little girl twirling the ends of the scarf between her fingers.

Sarah gave Noah one last look before heading out the door to deal with her latest roadblock.

CHAPTER 10

Sarah got out of her van and headed into the office of the electric company with her cup of coffee in hand. After leaving the school, she headed straight for the coffee shop to get her daily dose of caffeine.

When she stepped inside the office, she noticed the décor had changed little. The only difference she noticed was the once yellow walls now painted a cold shade of gray.

Her shoes were muffled on the wood laminate flooring and the scent of cleaning supplies hung heavy in the air.

There were only two seats along the wall with a small side table between them laden with old Field and Stream and Woman's Day magazines. Music played through the overhead speakers.

Sarah stepped up to the receptionist and set her coffee cup on the tall countertop.

The receptionist stopped typing on the computer and stood to face Sarah with a smile. She was in her sixties, with short gray hair and soft brown eyes. She wore tan slacks along with a matching black twin set. "May I help you?"

"I hope so. My name is Sarah Williams, and my electricity was off when I woke up this morning. I thought the rest of the grid on Laurel Cove was down, but as I was driving out of the neighborhood, I noticed other people had electricity."

"Let me check my computer." She sat down and glanced up at her as she typed. "Sarah Williams, is that correct?

"Yes ma'am. And my address is 164 Laurel Cove."

The woman's fingers flew over the keyword, and within a few seconds, she had an answer.

She printed something off and placed the piece of paper on the counter in front of Sarah. "It says here that your bill is three months overdue. Do you have a check stub where you mailed it in?" She gave Sarah a hopeful look.

Sarah opened her purse to pull out her checkbook. Just then, a familiar song came on over the speakers. It was a Kelly Clarkson song that she'd always get requests to sing in every venue she'd been in during her time traveling across America.

Sadness seeped into her chest. That life was over. Her new reality consisted of unpaid light bills, little boy issues, and burned chicken dinners. Tears burned behind her eyes, threatening to spill onto her cheeks.

Her elbow knocked over her cup, spilling coffee all over the countertop.

"I'm so sorry," Sarah grabbed the upturn cup and set it right. She dug in her purse for some napkins to clean up the mess, but she had nothing.

The receptionist grabbed a roll of paper towels from a drawer in her desk and quickly mopped up the mess.

"I hope I didn't ruin any paperwork on your side of the counter."

"Nothing's harmed. Accidents happen." She gave Sarah a reassuring smile.

"Good." Sarah pulled out her checkbook and looked through the register.

"The last notation I made of a check is November twenty-third. Is there any way that the bill didn't get sent to me?" She bit her lip.

"Let me do a little more digging." The receptionist continued to type and then printed something off. She stood and placed the paper in front of Sarah on the counter.

"It says here that in December, January and February, we mailed the statements." She pointed to the paper. "And you can see where there was a late notice on each."

Sarah rubbed her temple. "I always pay bills when they come in. Maybe with everything going on, I missed these."

The receptionist gave her a friendly smile. "That's okay. We can get you caught up today and have your electricity turned back on before you get home."

Sarah sighed with relief. "Thank you. That would be great." She looked at the woman and smiled. "You've been very helpful. I really appreciate it. You're much nicer than the last receptionist I talked to today."

"That receptionist wouldn't be Carol, from the school, would it?"

Sarah gaped. "How did you know?"

"Because she's my cousin. I'm Rita. Our moms were sisters, and they were as different as night and day, just like us."

"That must make Carol night and you day," Sarah blurted out.

Rita laughed. "Thanks for the compliment."

"Sorry, I know she's your family and all..." Sarah swallowed. She really didn't want to offend Rita. "I have a bad habit of blurting things out sometimes. It's something I'm working on."

"I'm not offended, Sarah." Rita cocked her head. "Your parents were Keith and Layla."

"Yes, they were."

"Oh, honey, I didn't recognize you. I went to church with your parents, and I played tennis with Layla on Wednesday mornings. I'm so sorry about your parents. They were wonderful people." Rita gave her a sincere smile.

"Thank you."

"How are you doing? You're back here raising your brother, right?"

"I am. And it's challenging. But we are doing the best we can."

"Well, if you need anything, let me know. In the meantime, I'm going to put a rush order on getting your electricity back on."

"That would be wonderful. And since I'm here, can I just set up automatic withdrawal so I don't have to worry about mailing a check?"

"Sure can. Let me get your banking information, and I'll get it all set up for you." Rita smiled.

After Sarah let the electric company, she drove over to the coffee shop for a large coffee. She missed her caffeine that morning, and she needed the extra energy to get through what the day held in store for her. At this rate, anything was possible.

CHAPTER 11

"Where is the camping stuff?" Sarah called down from the attic to Johnny, who was standing at the bottom of the stairs.

"How do I know? Dad always put it up there."

"Well, why don't you come up here and help me look?" She glared.

"I'm not coming up there. It's too scary."

"The only thing scary up here are the dust bunnies." She glanced around the crowded attic, wondering why her mom never cleared it out.

"Johnny?" She glanced down the stairs. He was gone. "You know this is for your camping trip. You should be helping." She cocked her head but heard nothing. He was probably hiding out in his room playing that stupid Nintendo Switch their parents had given him for his birthday.

"Figures." She opened some plastic bins, looking for something that resembled camping equipment, but found her yearbooks instead. She pulled out the one from her senior year and flipped through the pages.

She stilled when she saw her senior picture. *"Voted most likely to be a star."*

Sarah slammed the pages shut and tossed the book back into the plastic bin. She was foolish to believe she could make a career out of her singing.

She moved the box off the shelf and found a box with a blow up mattress. She pulled the box down and blew the dust off the top.

She fanned her hand to clear the air and tossed the box into the middle of the floor. She had a mattress, now she needed to find the tent.

After opening every plastic bin in the attic, she finally found the one that contained the tent and camping gear. She moved the box beside the mattress and opened it up. She found a tent along with two sleeping bags along with some outdoor kitchen items.

Noah had called her with a list of things she and Johnny would need for the Cub Scout camping trip. They would cook over a campfire so she wouldn't need the stove. She took that out of the box but kept the tin coffee mug. Noah better make good on his promise that she would have coffee when she woke up. She could do without a lot of things, but coffee definitely wasn't one of them.

The door to the attic slammed shut. She spun around and fisted her hands.

"Johnny, stop messing around. Don't think you can try to scare me. Remember, I don't believe in aliens or monsters." She marched over to the door and tried the knob.

It didn't budge.

Anger flared behind her eyes. "Look, you get over here and unlock this door right now, or else."

She waited for his response to her threat.

Silence.

"Okay fine. When I get out of here, you are going to be grounded. Which means no TV or video games," she seethed.

Just then, the doorknob turned.

She propped her hands on her hips and smirked.

The door flew open and there, standing in front of her, was Uncle Oliver.

"Uncle Oliver?" she gaped. "What are you doing here?"

"Rescuing you from the looks of things." He gave her a smile. "What are you doing up here?"

"I'm getting the stuff for our camping trip." She narrowed her eyes. "I thought you were in Seattle?"

"I was. But I have some vacation time, and I figured I'd come check on you and Johnny." He glanced down at the doorknob. "Looks like I got here just in time. What did you do? Lock yourself inside?"

"No. Johnny locked me in here," she brushed past him. "Where is he? I need to have a talk with him." She was going to ground that kid until he learned his lesson.

She bounded down the stairs and headed into the

kitchen. "Johnny," she called out but didn't see him. She headed to his room, but he wasn't there either.

She glanced out the window in the backyard. Johnny was chasing Phoenix around the large tree and laughing.

"I see things are going well?" Oliver followed her.

Ignoring him, she headed outside. "Johnny. Come here."

Johnny looked over at her and his smile faded. "What? I'm playing with Phoenix."

Tired of waiting for him to come to her, she stomped over to him. "Listen to me. Never lock me in the attic again. Do you understand?"

"I didn't lock you in the attic." He scowled.

"Johnny…"

Johnny looked past her, and his expression changed. "Uncle Oliver!"

"Come, give your uncle a hug!" Oliver knelt down and held out his arms.

Wearing a big smile, Johnny ran straight into Uncle Oliver's waiting arms.

"I didn't know you were coming." Johnny pulled back and smiled. "Did you bring me something?"

"Sure did." Uncle Olivier stuck his hand in the inside of his jacket pocket and pulled out a tiny model car. "This is a Lamborghini. I drove one like this when I went to Italy. It's the fastest car there in the world."

"No. it's not," Sarah muttered under her breath.

Uncle Oliver's gaze flickered over to her, but he said nothing.

"Wow, thanks!"

"We can't visit for too long. We are going camping tonight with the Cub Scouts."

"That sounds like fun. I remember when I was a Cub Scout. I loved camping and singing campfire songs." Uncle Oliver stood and gave them both grins.

"Can you come with us?" Johnny gave him a hopeful look.

"I'm afraid there's a sign-up sheet for who can go. He didn't get his name on it in time. Maybe Uncle Oliver can go next time." Sarah pulled out her phone and checked the time. "Speaking of time, we need to get our stuff packed."

Johnny sighed heavily and knelt down to give Phoenix a hug around the neck. "I don't want to go. Ben will not be there."

"Who's Ben?" Uncle Oliver asked.

"My best friend. His grandpa died, so he had to go to the funeral. I won't have any fun without Ben."

"How about if I just drop in and say hello to your Pack?"

"Will you?" Johnny's face brightened.

Sarah's stomach tightened. "I don't know if that's a good idea…"

"I ran into Noah Ellington and he said it was fine." Uncle Oliver grinned. "I won't spend the night since I don't have a sleeping bag. And I'll be here when you guys get back tomorrow with a home cooked meal."

Uncle Oliver was expecting to spend the night at

their house. Sarah fought to keep her expression neutral.

"Yay!" Johnny jumped. "I'm going to get packed for camping." Just like that, he ran inside the house.

"I hope you don't mind me spending the night. I didn't have time to get a hotel room."

"Sure. Besides, it's only for a night." Sarah forced a smile.

When he didn't confirm her statement, a small unease rested in her gut.

She couldn't think about that right now. Right now, she had a kid to take camping.

CHAPTER 12

*S*arah pulled into the campsite and killed the engine. When Johnny spotted some boys, he knew from his class, he sprinted out of the van, leaving her to unpack.

Sighing, Sarah slid out of the driver's seat. She glanced down at what she was wearing. Cut off denim shorts, Camo T-shirt, and hiking boots with appropriate black socks. Her fashion sense won out in the end and she had worn her camel-colored hat as well. She walked around to the side of the van, opened the door, and pulled out the large bin with the camping gear.

"Hey!" Noah jogged over to her. "Let me give you a hand."

"Thanks." She let him take the bin. She grabbed the snack bag and backpack she'd brought with her. "Looks like a good turnout, huh?"

"It is. All twelve of the boys came. We had a couple

of chaperones back out, so it's great that you could make it." He walked over to a spot marked off as Johnny's to set the bin down.

She looked over at the picnic tables where the boys were chasing each other around while the dads were setting up the tents.

"I didn't have time to look at the weather. Hope it doesn't rain because I forgot to pack rain jackets."

Noah smiled. "Clear weather all weekend. You should be good. Although I think you might get cold in those." He pointed to her cutoff denim shorts and grinned. "And I think the hat is a bit much for camping."

"I brought jeans just in case. And I'm wearing the hat because I didn't fix my hair today." She smirked.

He took the lid off her bin and looked up at her. "How did you ever survive living in a van for so long? Didn't you ever want to just find a house where you could stretch out and breathe?"

She laughed while pulling out the tent and tent stakes. "I can stretch out plenty in my van. Besides, I like the coziness of living tiny."

"Sounds like…"

A boy came running over to him. "Mr. Noah, Mark found a snake by the tree. He says it's not poisonous and he's going to pick it up."

Noah's eyes widened. He dropped what he was doing and raced toward the group of boys who were huddled together, studying the ground.

Sarah paused her tasks until Noah got over there

and assessed the situation. He urged the boys back and began talking and teaching them about safety and snakes, including how it's a good idea never to pick up a snake, even if it wasn't poisonous.

She smiled. Noah was pretty good at being the Cub Scout leader.

Assured the boys, and Johnny, were safe, Sarah went back to unrolling the tent.

"Need any help?"

Sarah looked up from where she was kneeling on the ground. A middle-aged man with a balding head and brown eyes smiled down at her. He was wearing a black T-shirt, jean shorts, which reached his knees, and tall white socks with his gray sneakers.

"I'm a whiz at setting up a tent." He stuck his thumbs in his shorts and rocked back on his heels.

"I appreciate the offer, but I think I can handle it."

"The ground out here is really rocky, and I don't think you'll be able to drive your stake into the ground."

She could almost hear what he was going to say next in her head. "You need a big, strong man to help you."

She stood and met his gaze. "Which one is your tent?"

He shoved his thumb over his shoulder. "The one closest to the trees."

"You mean the one that is about to blow away?"

He blinked, lost the smile, and spun around.

The wind had picked up and two of the tent pegs

had come out of the ground. The tent was flapping around wildly.

"Harvey, your tent is in trouble." Another dad stepped up and scratched his beer belly. "You might need to hammer it in better."

Forgetting all about her, Harvey hurried over to his tent. When he got there, he called for Mark, who she assumed was his son, to come help him. She watched as a boy ran over to where Harvey was.

"I'm Stanley. You must be new. Which one is your son?" Stanley swiped the sweat beading on his forehead with his hand and replaced his North Carolina Tar Heels baseball cap on his head.

"None. I'm Sarah. And Johnny Williams in my brother. I'm his legal guardian."

Stanley's expression changed to sympathy, and he nodded. "I heard about your parents. Hated that happened to them. Johnny's a good kid. My son is Allen. He's the one over there digging up earthworms. He's hoping we will get to go fishing."

"Is there a lake here?"

"A small pond through the woods." Stanley pointed toward a trail. "Which reminds me, I need to get my fishing pole and tackle out of the back of the truck. Let me know if you need anything." Stanley headed toward the direction of his truck.

Noah let out a whistle, and everyone turned.

"I need your attention, please. First, get your tent set up. If that's done, then you need to come with me and we will start gathering firewood. It's going to be dark soon. We need to get a fire started and gather enough wood for the entire night. After that, we are going to get dinner ready. I hope everyone is ready for a weekend of fun!"

The boys let out squeals and yells of excitement.

Sarah smiled. Maybe this weekend would be a good time for her and Johnny to grow closer.

With renewed enthusiasm, she bent down to finish setting up her tent. She hummed to herself as she worked. When she was done, she stood up and stretched her back to admire her work.

"That looks pretty good." Noah walked up beside her with his arms loaded with tree limbs.

"Thanks, I..." Her words drifted off as she spotted Uncle Oliver pull up to the campsite.

Just like that, her good mood was gone.

CHAPTER 13

Sarah shoved herself off the tree she'd been leaning against and glanced down at the time on her phone. She gritted her teeth and stifled her irritation.

Noah got up from the log where he'd been sitting around the campfire and walked over to her. "Everything okay? I noticed you didn't eat much at dinner?"

"I'm fine. Just wondering how much longer he's going to be here." Her gaze lingered on Uncle Oliver, who had the rapt attention of all the Cub Scouts who gathered around him, while he told of yet another grand adventure of being lost in the jungles of Costa Rica.

Noah followed her gaze. "If you didn't want him here, why did you invite him?"

She narrowed her eyes at him. "I didn't invite him. He invited himself."

Noah looked back at her. "Well, it will be bedtime

soon. And since he didn't bring a tent, he'll have to leave. Unless he plans on spending the night in his fancy convertible."

Sarah glanced over at the Mercedes. What kind of work was Uncle Oliver doing that he could afford such a luxury? The last time he'd visited her parents, he asked her mother for money to tide him over until he got back on his feet. Apparently, he followed through on his promise and had done well for himself.

"I don't care where he spends the night, as long as it's not here."

"I take it you're not close." Noah arched his brow. "I never heard you mention your uncle when we were in school."

She shoved her hands in her pocket and walked away from the group. Noah followed. "That's because I only saw him when he showed up to ask my mom for something." She cut her eyes at Noah. "There is something about him I don't trust. He's too … perfect."

Noah frowned. "What do you mean?"

"When he showed up at my house earlier, he was wearing pressed slacks and a button-down shirt with loafers. Now he's wearing those green shorts, tan short-sleeve shirt and that stupid hat. The fool looks like he is on a safari in Africa."

Noah snorted.

She jerked her head in his direction and scowled. "This isn't funny. He's trying to make everyone think he's perfect." She looked back at Uncle Oliver. "And make me look bad," she muttered.

Noah shook his head. "Sarah, I highly doubt that. He just wants to spend some time with you and Johnny, that's all." He gave her an encouraging smile. "I wouldn't worry about him. He'll be gone soon enough. He has a job to go back to."

Sarah studied Noah. "He didn't tell you what he did for a living, did he?"

Noah looked confused. "He said he owned a string of successful businesses."

"What? Don't you need a business degree for that?" She studied Uncle Oliver while he animatedly entertained the boys and their fathers with yet another tall tale, no doubt.

"Not necessarily. Someone that is business savvy can become very successful. One guy I met in college started out with a food truck. A year later he had several. Five years after that, some bigwig in New York bought his entire business for seven million dollars. Not bad for someone who hasn't hit thirty yet."

"Some people are lucky, I suppose." Her gut twisted at how unfair fate had turned out to be. Why did others have their dreams come true and not her?

"Wish I could find something that pays like that." She sighed heavily.

Noah cocked his head. "What exactly is your skill set? Besides being an independent world traveler and nature enthusiast."

Sarah smiled at the compliment. "Not exactly a world traveler. Maybe one day, though." She shoved her hand through her hair and looked up at the night sky. "That's just it. There are no job opportunities in Hopeton for the one thing I'm good at."

"Singing." Noah nodded his head.

She looked at him and felt a lump rising in her throat. Those dreams of hers were in the past. No use focusing on them now. "Know of anyone hiring?"

"Well, they need a new vet in town."

She grinned. "Don't think that's in my wheelhouse."

Noah grinned and nodded. "Have you tried the Green Thumb Nursery? Looks like Bernice is getting pretty busy."

"Bernice has Carolina, and she said Bernice isn't interested in hiring any more help. Besides, I don't know how well I'd get along with Bernice. I already checked at the diner and Getty said they aren't hiring." Sarah sighed heavily.

Stanley walked over to where they were standing. "Did I overhear that you need a job?"

Sarah wanted to say no, that he'd misunderstood. But she was in no position to pretend.

"Sarah is looking." Noah offered.

"Is that right?" Stanley grinned. "Well, it just so happens that I'm hiring. Do you have any experience being a receptionist?"

"No. What kind of business do you own, Stanley?

"I have a garage. I'm a mechanic."

Working at a garage wouldn't be that difficult, could it?

Sarah gave him a dubious look. "What exactly would I be doing?"

"Answering the phone and making appointments for people who want their oil changed and tires rotated. Sometimes we get walk-ins and fit them in. We stay pretty busy."

"What happened to your last receptionist?"

"She ran off with my best mechanic." He scowled. "They moved all the way to Vegas and started their own business. Her leaving almost made me lose hope in humanity."

"She must have been a pretty good receptionist for you to take it so personally."

Stanley cringed. "She was the worst. I'm mad at her for stealing my best mechanic."

Noah snorted, and Sarah bit down on her lip to keep from smiling. She had the distinct feeling that Stanley would not appreciate her amusement at his misfortune.

"Anyway, if you're interested, come by the garage after you drop Johnny off. It's called the Auto Doctor off Poplar Avenue."

They watched Stanley make his way over to the picnic table to the marshmallows, chocolate bars, and graham crackers. After dinner, Noah had promised the boys they could make smores.

"What do you think? Are you interested in working for Stanley?" Noah studied her.

"I don't...."

Uncle Oliver appeared out of nowhere. "What are you guys talking about? Sounded like you are looking for a job, Sarah? I wasn't aware you were out of work?

Do you need some money?" Her uncle's eyebrows drew together in a look of concern.

"I'm perfectly fine. I don't need anything from you." Sarah tried to make the words sound pleasant, but failed miserably. "I was just offered a job."

"You were?" Uncle Oliver looked surprised. "Where?"

"Working at Stanley's garage. He told me to start on Monday."

"You? Working in a garage?" he chuckled.

"Yes, a garage. It's not like I don't know how to answer the phone and book an oil change appointment. Now, if you will excuse me, I need to make sure the sleeping bags are ready." She marched over to her tent, wanting to curl her fingers into fists, but didn't want Uncle Oliver to know how much he got under her skin.

He acted like she couldn't take care of her own brother.

She was going to show him, and hopefully, this time, she'd shut him up for good.

CHAPTER 14

Sarah got Johnny to read two more chapters of his book before bed. After making sure she settled her little brother into his sleeping bag, she stepped out of the tent and walked to the campfire. Everyone was already asleep in their tents.

She didn't mind. She was used to being alone.

She placed another piece of wood on the fire and sat down in a fold-out chair she'd brought from home. Sarah stared into the dancing flames and the glowing embers.

"Mind if I join you?" Noah asked.

She gave a slight grin. "Not at all."

Noah settled himself in the chair and stared at the fire. "Everything okay? You seem ... tense."

She sighed heavily. "Johnny is in a bad mood because I didn't beg Uncle Oliver to camp out."

Noah shrugged. "Not your fault. He had to get

permission from me, and I didn't give it. So don't worry about it."

She shook her head. "Maybe he should have stayed. At least then he wouldn't be snooping around our house. Plus, Johnny wouldn't be mad at me. Again." She cocked her head as she stared at the fire. "I'm tired of being the bad guy, Noah. No matter what I do, it's just not enough."

Noah reached over and pulled two water bottles out of the cooler beside his chair. He handed her one.

"Thanks." She unscrewed the top and took a drink of the ice-cold liquid.

"Let me ask you something. Have you truly settled on the fact that Hopeton is now your home?"

She narrowed her eyes. "What do you mean?"

"Maybe Johnny's not mad at you, just worried that you won't stick around. He's already lost his parents. He's probably worried about losing you."

She snorted. "I doubt that."

"Kids can sense things. Maybe if you tried setting down your roots here in Hopeton, then Johnny would feel more secure."

She shifted uncomfortably in her seat. "So, how do I show him I'm here to stay?"

"Get involved in the town. Like volunteering at Johnny's school. They need parents to run off papers or decorate the classroom. Heck, you could even bring donuts and coffee and set them in the teacher's lounge for all the elementary teachers."

Sarah thought for a second. "Since I'm starting that job on Monday, I won't have time for volunteering, but I can bring coffee and donuts." She looked at him. "What else?"

"You have a magnificent voice. You could join the choir at church."

"I haven't been to church since I was in high school."

"I'm betting Johnny is missing seeing his Sunday School teacher and his class."

Her shoulders slumped. "I didn't even think about that."

Noah reached over and took her hand, giving her a gentle squeeze. "Take baby steps. You'll find your way. I promise."

She smiled. "You know, just being around you makes me feel better."

His eyebrows shot up. "Is that so?"

She reached over and scratched his chin. "Must be the beard. It makes you look so wise."

He blinked and then let out a laugh.

"Be quiet out there," Stanley called out from his tent.

Sarah pressed her lips together tightly to stop laughing, but she couldn't stop the snort that escaped.

"We should get some sleep," Noah lowered his voice.

They both stood.

Sarah reached her arms over her head and

stretched. The dazzling array of tiny bright lights dotting the midnight-colored sky held her attention.

"I can't ever get used to that," she whispered

"What's that?" He followed her gaze upward.

"A night sky, away from the city lights. It always makes me feel so insignificant."

She felt his eyes on her. She glanced over at him. "I bet you think that's stupid."

His eyes narrowed slightly as he gazed at her. Something about the way he was looking at her almost made her heart want to tumble a little.

She looked away. Noah wasn't the kind of man to make her heart tumble. It was Noah. The smart guy in high school who liked algebra, drove under the speed limit, and wanted to arrive early.

She preferred music to numbers, drove way too fast, and was usually late.

"Stupid is not how I would describe you. You are one of the most determined and intelligent people I know."

Sarah turned to him and blinked. She felt the blush steal across her cheeks at the intensity in his brown eyes.

"I should go to bed. We've got a long day tomorrow." She gathered her drink.

Noah stood and shoved his hands in his jeans pocket. "It is getting late."

She swallowed and forced a smile. "Good night, Noah." She walked toward her tent.

"Good night, Sarah."

She slipped inside her tent and toed off her shoes.

Quietly, she slipped inside her sleeping bag and tried to forget about how Noah had looked at her with those ardent eyes that seemed to pry into her soul.

CHAPTER 15

Sarah could tell that dawn was approaching through the tiny opening of the tent. The light outside was slowly turning from pitch black to purple. The birds, still huddled in their nest, were still quiet, but she knew within the hour they would be awake and singing.

She crawled out of the sleeping bag, jostling the blow-up mattress she had shared with Johnny. She scrounged around for her jeans and slipped them on, then peeked through the nylon opening and sighed with relief when she spotted Noah making coffee over the campfire.

She quickly slipped on her hiking boots and made her way over to him.

"Thank God," she breathed out. The welcome aroma of fresh coffee in the early morning air made her heart almost sing.

Noah looked up at her and smiled. "I'm the one making coffee, not Him."

She grinned. "Look at you, making jokes."

He poured her a cup of coffee, handed her the tin cup, and stood. "I'm not the same nerd in high school you thought I was."

Sarah frowned as she wrapped her hands around the mug. "I never thought you were a nerd. Besides, what did it matter what I thought?" She took a sip. She sighed with contentment as the dark coffee slid down her throat. The cool breeze seemed to caress her face and ruffle her loose hair.

"It mattered."

She cut her eyes at him, confused by his answer. Intrigued, she opened her mouth, but he cut her off.

"I need to get the boys up. We have a long day of hiking, fishing, and geocaching before dinner tonight." He wiped his hands on his dark pants and pointed at the picnic table. "There is creamer in the cooler if you want it."

"Thanks." She watched as he made his way to the tent closest to them and let all the boys know it was time to get up.

Sarah headed over to the picnic table and added some creamer to her black coffee. She took a seat at the table, enjoying the quiet of the morning. The campground was nearly empty. She bet no one wanted to camp next to a group of loud third graders and had not booked a site.

She couldn't blame them.

Being outdoors, in the peace and quiet, was one of her favorite things.

Harvey was the first adult to pop his head out of the tent. He grimaced as he looked around, but immediately brightened when he spotted Sarah. He scurried back into his tent before reappearing in cargo shorts and a sleeveless T-shirt two sizes too small.

"Good morning." He smiled and glanced at her cup. "Is there any more of that?"

She forced a smile, irritated that her peaceful morning had been interrupted. "By the campfire. Noah was making it when I got up."

Harvey grabbed a Styrofoam cup off the picnic table and poured himself a cup of coffee. He slurped loudly and then let out a boisterous sigh.

"How'd you sleep? You probably aren't used to being out here in the big wilderness." Harvey's voice carried through the campground.

Sarah tightened her fingers on the tin cup and tamped down her irritation. "I slept very well," she lowered her voice, "except for the snoring coming out of your tent."

Harvey didn't seem to hear her last statement. He walked over and sat down on the picnic bench beside her. The seat shuddered under his weight.

Sarah tensed and planted her feet on the ground, ready to stand up if the bench suddenly gave way.

"I always love the outdoors. Something about sleeping under the stars and the ability to survive off the land makes a man feel more like a man." Harvey lifted his chin.

Stanley crawled out of his tent and stretched his arms over his head. "Harvey, you wouldn't survive a day alone in the woods. You couldn't even make the campfire last night. Noah had to do that. And don't forget about the great job you did setting up your tent," Stanley teased with a snicker.

Harvey narrowed his eyes at Stanley. "Well, if you hadn't gathered green wood for the fire, it would have started right away. And the only reason my tent came out of the ground was some of those boys must have pulled the tent peg out, you know, to prank me."

Sarah stood to get a refill of the coffee. She needed to put some distance between her and the stench of testosterone that hung heavy in the air.

"Those boys were nowhere near your tent. The smell alone would choke a pig. You probably should have laid off the beans last night." Stanley laughed.

Harvey's face went beet red. He jerked his head in her direction.

Sarah cut her eyes away from the men, studying the contents of her mug.

"You're just jealous because the boys didn't like your campfire story you told last night. They liked mine better."

"We'll see how well you survive today. We are going fishing, so let's see how many fish you catch." Stanley snorted.

Noah walked up and eyed the two men. "Everything okay?"

"I think everyone is hungry." Sarah spoke up, changing the subject. "What is on the menu for breakfast?"

"We are having campfire breakfast burritos."

"Sounds good." Stanley licked his lips, his feud with Harvey quickly forgotten.

Noah nodded at Harvey and Stanley. "You two can make sure the boys are up and going. Sarah, if you don't mind, you can help with breakfast."

"Perfect." She followed Noah over to the picnic table.

Harvey and Stanley parted ways and went from tent to tent, making sure the boys were up.

"Do they always argue like that?" She cut her eyes at Noah.

"Yes, but they seem more competitive since you're here. They are clearly trying to impress you."

She cringed. "They're old enough to be my dad."

Noah barked out a laugh. "Sarah, men never stop trying to impress beautiful women. It's in our DNA."

She felt herself blush at the compliment.

Sarah cleared her throat. "So what do I do?"

"I tried to prep as much ahead of time as possible. Look in the cooler, and you'll find the plastic container of eggs that I already cracked and whipped."

She opened the lid of the Yeti cooler and pulled out the container of eggs. "Do you want this sausage too?" She held up a plastic container of cut-up sausage.

"Yes. We'll cook both together in the skillet over the campfire. Once we get these cooked together, we'll put them in aluminum foil packets with some cheese and set them on coals."

"Sounds like you've done this before."

He grinned. "I have with Nathalie. I do these over the firepit in our backyard."

"You should have brought her. She would have liked this." Sarah busied herself pouring the eggs and sausage into the skillet.

"She doesn't like to be around boys much. Not after what happened with her hair."

Sarah narrowed her eyes. "About that. Did the boy's parents contact you and apologize?"

"They did. They said he was grounded from his Nintendo Switch."

"That doesn't sound very harsh."

Noah barked out a laugh from where he was stoking up the fire. "You obviously don't understand boys."

"I won't argue with that." She poured the eggs and sausage into the skillet and took it to the campfire. The wind picked up, and the smoke changed directions. She darted out of the way before it could encompass her. "So, what are we going to do after breakfast?" She sat down in a chair near the campfire and sipped on her coffee.

"We are going to work on one of our badges. It's called Baloo the Builder. I brought some sticks that the boys are going to strip the bark off to make hiking sticks."

She arched a brow. "You're going to let a bunch of third graders loose with a pocket knife?"

He looked up at her and grinned. "They've already earned their whittling badge and know about knife safety. Besides, the adults will watch over them while they work."

"What else is on the agenda?" She took a sip of her coffee. She grimaced and reached for the hot pot to refresh her tepid drink.

"We are going to work on our Fur, Feathers, and Fern badge. While we hike, they need to identify six signs of animals living near where we are hiking." Noah pointed toward the trail leading to the pond. "I already scouted it out this morning. We should find something there."

"Sounds easy enough."

Noah grinned. "That's the thing. It sounds easy enough with a checklist, but throw in twelve different boys, and it's hard to keep them all on the same page." He motioned at her cup. "Better drink up. You'll need all the caffeine you can hold to keep up with them."

She laughed, but the way he was staring at her made her believe he was completely serious.

Gripping her coffee tin tight, she downed the contents.

CHAPTER 16

Sarah watched in amazement as the boys wolfed down the breakfast burritos. Even Johnny had two. The recipe was easy enough, and she made a mental note to make these for her brother when they got home. Surely she couldn't mess up this recipe.

After breakfast, everyone cleaned up the campsite and tossed their trash. Noah tasked Stanley with the duty of cleaning the cast-iron skillet. Stanley grumbled under his breath but did the chore, anyway.

"I would have washed the skillet," she whispered to Stanley.

"You have already pulled your weight." He cut his eyes at Stanley and Harvey. "They have not. It's like watching toddlers. Getting into things and crying when they are hungry."

She couldn't help but grin. She liked the fact that

Noah didn't expect her to clean up just because she was a woman.

"So what's next?" She rocked back on her heels in her hiking boots, stuck her pink baseball cap on her head, and tossed her long braid to the side. After breakfast, she had changed back into her shorts and threw on a black T-shirt.

"We are whittling." Noah flashed her a white smile.

She groaned. What if one of them cut off a finger?

"Don't worry. They have all earned their whittling badges and know the rules. We are just going to watch and make sure they are being slow and safe while working their walking sticks."

She bit her lip. She wasn't as confident as Noah was in their abilities.

"All right, scouts! I want everyone to walk over to the back of my truck to pick out a stick. Once you've done that, come back over and have a seat on the ground."

The boys raced over to the bed of his Dodge truck and pulled out sticks.

One boy, Jake, had chosen a stick, but when he saw Johnny's stick, he tried to take it away.

Sarah lifted her chin and walked over to the boys. "Everything okay here?"

"No fair, his stick is longer." Jake scowled as he pointed to Johnny's hiking stick.

"No, it's not," Johnny argued.

"Yes, it is. I want that stick." Jake reached out for Johnny's stick, but Johnny backed away.

"Here, let me have both of the sticks." Sarah held out both hands.

Johnny sighed but reluctantly handed his over. Jake narrowed his eyes at her before finally relenting.

She held them up. "See, they are both the same size." She handed Johnny's stick back to him. Her brother took it and headed over to the picnic table where the boys were sitting.

"Take your stick and head over to the other boys." She held out the stick to Jake.

"Eww. Gross. I don't' want that stick. It's got your cooties all over it," he snarled. He grabbed another stick out of the back of the truck and ran over to the boys.

She bit back a reply. She wondered if he was this rude with his parents.

Noah looked over at her from his position at the picnic table. He gave her a questioning look.

She plastered a smile on her face. The last thing she wanted was for him to think she couldn't handle a smart-mouth kid.

Sarah wandered over just as Noah began giving instructions on the proper way to whittle their walking stick.

"When is the fishing trip, Noah?" Stanley shot Noah a look.

Sarah stood near Johnny. She was pretty impressed that he took his time and did not hurry, as he made precise cuts to his walking stick.

"We'll head out fishing closer to noon. The boys will work on their walking sticks. Then we will head off to identify some animals along the trail toward the lake." Noah hovered over each boy, making sure they were being as safe as possible with their pocket knife.

She noticed Jake wasn't as careful as the other boys. "It's not a race," she reminded him.

He didn't bother looking up, but narrowed his eyes as he cut another slice into the wood.

"What about lunch? I can't miss lunch. My blood sugar will drop." Harvey scratched his enormous belly and frowned.

"Harvey, you use that excuse every time you think you're going to miss a meal." Stanley shot back.

"I do not. I have a medical condition." Harvey lifted his chin.

"If stupidity were a medical condition, you would be the poster boy." Stanley snorted.

"Why you…" Harvey fisted his hands at his side.

"Why don't we give each other some distance?" Sarah suggested, looking at Noah for backup. The last thing she wanted was for one of the boys to have an accident and get cut.

"She's right, guys. Everyone stand up and take two steps away from the nearest person next to you." Noah spoke with authority. The boys grumbled but obeyed.

She looked at Noah and mouthed the words, thank you.

He gave her a slight grin.

"Stanley, do you mind getting the fishing gear ready? We'll take it with us on our hike."

Stanley brightened. "Sure will." With a smile, he went over to the back of his truck to gather the supplies.

"What about me?" Harvey looked a bit dejected.

"I'd like you to grab that big cooler out of my truck. Make sure it's loaded with drinks and sandwich meat, and we'll take it with us to the pond."

Harvey nodded enthusiastically, relieved he wouldn't starve to death on the cub scout camping trip.

"What about me?" Sarah propped her hands on her hips.

"Would you mind taking my big hiking bag and filling it with the bread and chips that I left in the front seat of my truck?"

"Not at all. As long as you have everything covered here?" She didn't take her eyes off Johnny.

"I'll watch them." Noah moved closer to Johnny as he kept watch over all the boys.

She relaxed enough, knowing Noah would monitor Johnny.

Sarah walked over to his truck and found the hiking bag in the back seat. She opened the passenger's side door, grabbing the sandwich bread with the chips and loaded them into the bag. Slinging the hiking bag over her shoulder, she walked back to the boys.

Stanley and Harvey were there, ready to move on to the next scout activity.

"All right, guys. From the looks of things, everyone did a great job. So carefully fold your pocket knife, and hand them back to me." Noah held out his hand, as each boy placed their pocket knife into the palm of his hand. He put them in a zip-lock bag and then into a pocket of the hiking bag Sarah was holding. He took the bag from her and put it on his shoulders.

"Okay, now we are going to be doing two things at once. We are going to be looking for traces of animals on the trail. So you might find a feather, or a tooth…"

"Or some poop," one boy called out. The boys erupted in laughter.

"And do you know what bear poop is called?"

No one answered. Noah looked at Harvey, and Stanley, but both men weren't paying attention. Stanley was fixing the hook on one of the fishing poles while Harvey was busy rifling through the cooler, trying to grab a soda.

"Sarah? Do you know?" Noah arched his brow and waited.

"Scat."

"No, it's not." Jake scowled.

"Actually, Sarah is right. Bear poop is called scat." Noah gave Jake a pointed look.

The boys all looked at her like she was growing a flower out of the top of her head.

"How do you know that? You're a girl." Jake's mouth dropped.

Once again, she tamped down her anger. "I camp a lot. So I know a lot about the outdoors."

"Oh yeah? Have you ever seen bigfoot while you're camping?" Zack cocked his head.

"No. But I saw a pack of wolves in Yellowstone National Park."

"Did Johnny see them too?" Jake narrowed his eyes.

"No, he wasn't with me." Sarah frowned. This kid was getting on her last nerve.

"Then you probably didn't see them." Jake turned on his heel and walked over to the campfire, which now consisted of black coals and smoke.

"Jerk," Sarah muttered under her breath.

"Sorry about that. Boys can be…"

"Cruel?" She looked up at him.

"They can be childish." He squeezed her shoulder gently and gave her a smile.

"It's okay, Noah. I have tough skin." She reassured him.

"It's okay not to be strong all the time, Sarah." His words were soft. She wondered if he meant something else entirely.

"I guess we should be going." She took a step back.

He tore his gaze away from her and clapped his hands together. "Scouts, get your walking sticks. Let's form a line behind me and head into the woods. Remember to look out for tracks and alert me if you see something so we can stop and inspect."

The boys ran over to the picnic table, grabbing their walking sticks. Two of the boys elbowed each other to get first place behind Noah. After a stern look from him, they form an orderly line.

Harvey and Stanley got in line behind the boys, leaving her to bring up the rear.

Sarah didn't mind. At least she'd have some time to herself to reflect on her surroundings and try to ground herself.

CHAPTER 17

Sarah had been hoping for some peace, but all she got was an earful from Harvey and Stanley. Both men were trying to outdo the other with stories of how they were experts at fishing and hunting.

When Harvey had told her he'd seen a gorilla one time in the woods when he'd been hunting, Stanley laughed and told him he must have been drinking. And when Stanley said he'd caught an alligator one time when he'd been fishing in the Mississippi River, Harvey called him a liar.

By the time they made it to the pond to fish, Sarah was sick and tired of hearing them both talk.

She walked over to Johnny and knelt down beside him. "Need any help baiting your hook?

"Nah. I got it." He bit his lip and concentrated on putting the worm on the hook.

"He can't do it. His dad always put his worm on his hook," Jake snarled.

Sarah felt the slight burn of anger building inside of her. She glanced over at her brother. His shoulders slumped forward, and he cast his eyes on the ground.

"Jake," Noah warned.

"He knows how to bait a hook, Jake." Sarah narrowed her eyes at the boy.

"Yeah? Then why is he sitting over there crying like a baby?" Jake sneered.

Sarah jerked her head in Johnny's direction. He didn't bother looking up, but wiped his face with the back of his hand.

She headed over to Johnny and knelt down. "Are you okay?" She kept her voice quiet so the other boys couldn't hear.

"No." He looked up at her with large tears in his eyes and held up his hand. "I stuck the hook in my thumb."

She gasped and grabbed his hand. "Keep still."

"Look!" Jake pointed at Johnny's hand. "He's got a hook stuck in his thumb. He will have to go to the ER to get it cut out."

"I am?" Johnny looked at Sarah with terror in his eyes.

"Let me see." Harvey elbowed his way past the boys and bent down. "Dang. That has to hurt. I had a friend who had a hook in his thumb and they had to cut it off."

"The hook or the thumb?" Stanley asked as he looked over Sarah's shoulder.

Sarah looked at Harvey and gave him a warning look not to scare her brother.

Harvey scratched his head. "I don't remember."

She rolled her eyes.

Noah came over and knelt beside Johnny. "Let me see." He examined the wound carefully. "There's good news. You will not go to the ER. We can get it out."

"But it will hurt." Johnny shook his head.

"For just a second, but then it will feel much better." Noah gave him a reassuring smile. He looked up at Stanley. "Hand me some fishing line."

Stanley set the bag with the fishing supplies on the ground and opened it. He pulled out a spool of fishing line.

Noah took it and pulled out a pocket knife. After unrolling a long piece of line, he cut it.

"What are you going to do with that?" Sarah cocked her head. By this time, all the boys had forgotten about baiting their hooks and gathered around Johnny to watch the spectacle.

"Everyone back up," Noah looked at the boys. They let out a disappointed sigh, but obeyed and took a step back.

"This is a trick that I learned." He looked at Sarah. "Hold his hand still."

She tightened her hold on Johnny's hand while Noah began wrapping the fishing line tightly below the hook.

JODI ALLEN BRICE

"That hurts." Johnny whimpered.

"Can anyone tell me what kind of bird that is in the tree?" Noah focused his attention on the hook while the boys looked up in the treetops.

"It's a finch," Jake called out.

"Not it's not. It's a cardinal." Sammy said.

"You guys are looking at the wrong bird. I want to know what kind of bird is sitting on the branch over Mr. Harvey's head." Noah didn't take his eyes off as he wound the fishing line around Johnny's thumb.

Everyone, except Sarah and Noah, turned just in time to see a bluebird take flight.

"It's a Blue Jay," Johnny answered.

"Johnny is right. And the hook is out." Noah held up the freed hook in his hand.

"That didn't even hurt.' Johnny smiled.

"Good. Now we get to bandage it up and get on about our business of fishing." Noah pulled the first aid kit out of his backpack and began putting anti-septic on the wound. "There is hardly any blood, so I think you'll only need a band-aid." Noah carefully wrapped the thumb in a band-aid and smiled at Johnny.

"Can I go fish now?" He looked at Noah.

"Yes, but only if you let Stanley bait your hook."

Johnny nodded and grabbed his pole. He joined the other boys and adults standing near the edge of the water.

"Thank you." Sarah stood. "I've never seen anyone get a hook out like that."

"Saw it on YouTube." Noah grinned. "Don't tell the boys. I might lose some of my street cred."

She laughed and then grew serious. "Noah, can I ask you something?"

"Sure." He gathered his first aid supplies and put them back in his bag.

"Did Dad really not let Johnny bait his own hook?"

Noah shifted his weight. "Your Dad was overprotective with Johnny. Like all dads."

She stiffened. "No. Not like all Dads. When I was a kid, Dad wasn't like that at all. I can remember he gave me my independence. I mean, I knew how to drive by ten, could change a tire by eleven, and camped out by myself when I was thirteen. He didn't baby me." She glanced over at the water and narrowed her gaze on Johnny. A flash of resentment flashed through her.

"Your parents knew you had an independent streak." Noah cocked his head at her. "It wasn't like they loved you any less than Johnny."

She jerked her head back in his direction. "How do you do that?"

He frowned, clearly confused. "Do what?"

"Read my mind."

A small grin played on his lips. "I don't. I know you, Sarah. Besides, you're pretty easy to read."

She sighed heavily. "I was always told I don't have a poker face."

"No, you most definitely do not." He laughed. "Now, let's go catch some fish and watch Harvey and Stanley argue about who the better fisher is." He started over to where Jake desperately tried to get his fishing line out of a branch.

Sarah planted her hat firmly on her head, straightened her shoulders and marched over to Johnny, determined to shove away any unpleasant thoughts and focus on the moment.

$\mathcal{A}$fter working a full day at Stanley's auto garage, Sarah pulled into her driveway. She looked over at Johnny. "Dinner may be a little late tonight. I forgot to set some meat out to thaw before we left this morning. I had planned on making Hannah's meatloaf. But we're going to have to settle for frozen pizza."

"The last time you made pizza, you burned the cheese." Johnny scowled.

She opened her door and took a deep breath. "That's because I didn't set the timer and I got distracted. I promise, no burnt pizza tonight."

Johnny opened his door and slung his backpack on his shoulder. "Whatever. As long as it's not burned. It made my stomach hurt last time."

She got out of the van and followed him, where he was impatiently waiting for her to unlock the door.

He looked up at her. She could tell something was bothering him.

"What's wrong?" She asked as she fished the house key out of her purse.

"Where did Uncle Oliver go? He said he would be home to see us when we got back from camping on Saturday. He said he was going to cook a big dinner for us. When we got home, he was gone." Johnny looked up at her with sad eyes.

"I don't know. I suppose he had to go back to work." She stuck the key in the lock and turned the knob. The door swung open. "Now go grab a snack and we will get started on homework."

"I hate homework." Johnny hurried inside and made a beeline for the kitchen.

Sarah set her purse down on the entryway table and shut the door behind her. She, too, found it odd that Uncle Oliver had not been waiting for them when they got back home. She went through each room, carefully inspecting to make sure he hadn't stolen anything. Everything was in its place. Maybe he really was checking in with them to make sure they were okay.

She walked into the kitchen and found Johnny grabbing a handful of chocolate chip cookies out of the cookie jar.

"Hey, don't fill up on sweets. We'll be eating in a couple of hours."

He scowled and reluctantly put back one of the three cookies he had in his hand. She poured him a glass of milk and set it on the kitchen table.

She stifled a yawn, put the kettle on the stove, pulled down a mug from the cabinet, and found the tin of tea. The doorbell rang just as the kettle began to whistle.

"Who could that be?"

"Probably someone selling something. I'm going to my room." Johnny grabbed his cookies with the glass of milk and bounded upstairs.

Sarah shook her head and turned off the stove.

She headed to the door, taking her time and hoping whomever it was would be gone by the time she opened the door.

"I hope I'm not bothering you," Hannah said sweetly, holding two casserole dishes in her arms.

"If that's dinner, then no. You are definitely not bothering me. Come on in." She stood to the side as Hannah entered.

Hannah made her way into the kitchen and set the casserole dish on the counter. "I've made a chicken pot pie for dinner. And there is peach cobbler for dessert."

Sarah inhaled deeply at the wonderful aroma. "Hannah, you are a lifesaver."

Hannah laughed. "I don't know about that. Just helping a friend."

Sarah sighed heavily. "Thank you. It's appreciated. I didn't have time to thaw anything out before I left for work."

"How was your first day working for Stanley?"

Sarah grimaced, and then she pulled down a second mug. "Tea?"

"Yes, please." Hannah took a seat at the kitchen table.

Sarah poured the hot water over two tea bags of Earl Grey and set one mug in front of Hannah.

"The job itself is actually a good fit." She looked away.

Hannah narrowed her eyes as she dunked her tea bag in and out of the hot water. "I feel there's a 'but' in there somewhere."

Sarah nodded. "But I don't think Stanley likes me too much."

"Why would you feel like that?" Hannah frowned.

"Because I had two walk-ins. One was an elderly woman who said her car was making a weird growling noise when she turned the steering wheel. The mechanics were backed up for hours, so I went out to look at it. It turns out she was just low on power steering fluid so I filled it up for her and charged her for the fluid."

"That's great!" Hannah smiled.

"Stanley didn't think so. He was furious that I didn't book an appointment for her so he could have one of the mechanics do it and charge her for labor as well." Sarah took a sip and sighed.

"Well, you did the right thing. Was that the only thing he got upset about?"

"No. Another high school student came in worried to death. She kept hearing a noise, and I went out to look at it. She had a rock stuck in her tire tread. So I got it out. But I didn't tell Stanley about that potential customer. Who knows how much he would have charged her for that?"

"That's probably for the best. Besides, it only sounds like you only had one bad incident."

Sarah blew out a long breath. "Not really. Apparently, his wife didn't know that he had hired me. She came in to bring his lunch. When she saw me sitting behind the desk, she demanded to know who I was."

"Stanley didn't tell his wife he hired a receptionist?" Hannah frowned.

"No. And it didn't help that I'm twenty years younger than her. She told me I looked like a home wrecker and to stay away from Stanley." She shuddered. "As if I would even consider that old man."

Hannah leaned forward. "She didn't?"

"Yes, she did. And then she stormed off into the garage to find Stanley. You could hear them arguing in the office. We had two of the moms from Johnny's school waiting on their oil changes. I'm sure they heard everything."

"Oh, Sarah. I'm so sorry."

"Me, too" Her phone dinged with a text. She picked it up and read it. "You've got to be kidding me."

"What's wrong?"

"That was from Stanley. He said he has to let me go."

Hannah pressed her lips into a thin line. "Did he give you a valid reason?"

"He just said it wasn't working out. Which is code for his wife told him to fire me." Sarah pressed her face into her hands. "Now I'm back to square one. Jobless."

"That's not right." Hannah slammed her hand down on the table, making Sarah jump. "One stupid, spineless man is firing you for excelling in your job? That's not right at all."

Sarah smiled at her friend, sitting there like a petite, avenging angel.

"Hannah, it's okay. I promise. I've survived worse."

Hannah nodded. "I know you will. You're strong."

Sarah smiled at her. "Thanks for saying that."

"You didn't tell me how the camping trip went. Were the boys mesmerized by your beauty and camping skills?"

Sarah barked out a laugh. "Not at all. One, in particular, wouldn't touch a walking stick because it had my cooties on it."

They both laughed.

"I prefer camping solo, where I can enjoy nature's solitude and beauty, not have to deal with my little brother getting a hook stuck in his hand."

Hannah's smile faltered. "He got a hook in his hand? Is he okay?"

"He's fine. Thankfully, Noah got it out with some fishing line. He was pretty calm under the circumstances."

"Johnny or Noah?" Hannah took a sip of her tea.

Sarah smiled. "Both."

Johnny came bounding down the stairs. He brightened when he saw Hannah.

"Ms. Hannah! Did you bring me something?"

"Johnny, that's pretty rude. Ms. Hannah doesn't have to bring something just to come over to visit."

His face fell.

"Would you be disappointed if I just came to see you, Johnny?"

"No. But it would be nice to have some of your cookies like you made at Christmas."

Hannah set her tea down and placed her hands on her lap. "I didn't bring any cookies. But I brought dinner. Along with a dessert that I'm sure you'll love."

Delight spread across his face. He ran and flung himself in her arms, hugging her tightly.

"Thank you, Ms. Hannah."

She hugged him back. "Any time, Johnny."

Sarah looked away at the intimate moment between her brother and Hannah. He'd never hugged her like that. Nor had he shown her any gratitude.

Once again, she shook off the intrusive feelings and reminded herself that it didn't matter.

She was being unreasonable and needed to get a grip. She needed to be more like Noah, who didn't take offense so easily.

"I must go so you can get your homework done before dinner." Hannah stood to put her cup in the sink. "Thank you for the tea."

"Anytime. And thank you for dinner." Sarah smiled as she walked her neighbor to the door.

"It's no bother. I hope you both will enjoy it."

Hannah gave them one last wave before heading out the door.

Sarah closed the door and took a breath. "Now let's get out your homework and..." she turned just in time to see Johnny racing upstairs.

CHAPTER 19

*A*fter being fired on Monday, Sarah had used the rest of the week putting in applications in Hopeton. It wasn't until late Thursday that she got a call back from Johnny's principal, stating they were always looking for substitute teachers. In fact, the sixth grade teacher had the flu and called out for Friday, so they were desperate for help.

She didn't think she was the right fit as a teacher, but she knew beggars could not be choosers. So she reluctantly agreed.

"How do I look?" Sarah turned around and faced Johnny at the kitchen table.

He frowned. "Why are you so dressed up?"

She sighed. "Remember? I'm substituting at your school today. The sixth-grade teacher called out sick."

He shrugged. "You look fine." He went back to eating his sugary cereal.

She walked into the living room, and studied her

reflection in the mirror which hung over the brick fireplace.

She'd chosen a long pink floral maxi skirt and paired it with a white fitted T-shirt. She noticed the other teachers at school wore slacks, but she didn't own a pair, so she decided on the skirt.

She threw on her denim jacket and added some gold hoop earrings.

Now she needed to decide on shoes. She glanced at the time in the kitchen. "Finish eating and go brush your teeth." She didn't wait for a response from her brother as she hurried into her room.

Sarah opened her closet door and pulled out a pair of sneakers. Shaking her head, she tossed them over her shoulder. Next, she pulled out her hiking boots, and also decided against them as well. She had some dressy heels but knew her feet would be killing her by the end of the day.

Her gaze settled on a pair of red leather cowboy boots. "Yes!" she pulled them out of the closet and tugged them on.

Sarah took one final glance at her reflection in the mirror and decided she looked pretty good. Grabbing her fedora hat, she pulled it on. She might have to take it off during class, but if she had to go outside during recess, she'd put it back on to keep the sun out of her eyes.

"I'm ready." Johnny called out.

She raced out of her room, grabbing her bag and

keys to her van. She stopped in front of Johnny and held out her arms, waiting for his opinion.

"Well?" she asked.

"I don't think you can wear a hat to school. It's against the rules."

She rolled her eyes. "Of course, it is." She sighed heavily. "I'll take it off in the van. Let's get going. I'm supposed to be there early so Principal Wheeler can give me the schedule for today." She opened the front door, and he ran out to the van. She locked the door and followed him.

Sarah pulled into the school parking lot thirty minutes before the parents started lining up in the car line to drop off their kids.

Johnny didn't bother waiting for her but jumped out and started for the school entrance.

She grabbed her purse and hat and locked her door.

As she walked across the parking lot, she took in the landscaping at the school. The azalea bushes were in full bloom and the neatly manicured hedges were pristine. Without the noise of a full school, it actually looked quite peaceful.

She opened the door to find Johnny looking at one of the wall murals.

She stopped beside him and looked at the painting of a tree with different colored hand prints along the wall as leaves. Beneath the mural were the words, 'What will your beautiful hands do today?'

"That must be new. It wasn't here when I was in elementary class. It's a lot of hand prints. Must be from all the elementary kids." She looked at him. "Is your hand print here?"

"I wasn't here that day."

"Oh, yeah?" Sarah cocked her head, examining all the sizes of handprints. "Where were you?"

"At Mom and Dad's funeral."

Stunned, she turned to him. "Johnny…"

"Miss Williams. I see you have arrived." Carol's voice echoed in the hallway.

Sarah turned. "Yes, I was told to arrive early."

Carol's gaze swept up and down Sarah. Her lips pressed into a thin white line. "I see, you didn't inquire about the dress code."

Sarah's hackles went up. "Principal Wheeler said casual."

Carol waved her hand at Sarah's attire. "I wouldn't call that casual. That's more like what one might wear to a seedy bar."

Sarah looked down at her outfit and then back at Carol. She forced a bright smile. "Thanks, Carol."

Carol, clearly not amused, narrowed her eyes. "Follow me. Johnny, you go to your classroom. Mrs. Wallace is already here."

Johnny didn't bother telling Sarah goodbye. As soon as Carol uttered her words of dismissal, he darted down the hallway to his classroom.

"Traitor." Sarah muttered under her breath.

She followed Carol into Principal Wheeler's office.

The principal looked up from going over a file and gave her a brief smile. "Miss Williams. I'm so glad you could fill in today. We have two teachers out with the flu in the elementary school and the high school has three. It's the season for it, I suppose." She noticed Carol was still in the room. "Thank you, Carol. Can you please print out my schedule for next month?"

"I'll get right on it. "Carol shot one last glare in Sarah's direction before leaving.

"I have a strange feeling that Carol doesn't like me." Sarah deadpanned.

Principal Wheeler looked a bit flustered.

Until Sarah smiled.

Principal Wheeler let out a laugh. "Yes. She's totally old school. A couple of years ago, she brought up having the teachers wear uniforms."

"But the kids don't even wear uniforms." Sarah frowned.

"I know. I told her that the teachers would quit first. Anyway," she waved at the chair across the desk, "sit down and we will run over a quick list of what today's schedule is like."

"Okay." She eased into the chair, setting her purse and hat on the floor.

"You're substituting for Mrs. Gainsworth. She teaches sixth grade math."

She broke out in a cold sweat. "It's not algebra, is it?"

Principal Wheeler chuckled. "No. Not in sixth grade." She typed in something on the computer and then nodded. "According to her notes, they are currently learning measurements."

Sarah frowned. "Measurements?"

"Like how to measure all aspects of circles, prisms and pyramids."

Her stomach dropped.

"Don't worry. She emailed me some papers for you to make a copy of and have them do. She'll grade them when she gets back."

"So how many kids does she have in her class?"

Principal Wheeler printed something off at her desk and picked up the paper. "Her first period class has thirteen kids. Second period has the same amount. Third period she had free, so I suggest eating your lunch then, since you'll be on playground duty at noon."

She swallowed. "I will? What does that entail?"

"Watching the kids, making sure they don't hurt themselves or hurt others. You'll only be watching the second graders. Then after that, you have about an hour to get ready for your last class after lunch. You'll have about eighteen kids in that group." Principal Wheeler handed her the single piece of paper.

Sarah took it and studied it. "So I need to run off copies enough for all three classes?"

"Yes. Use the copier in the teachers' lounge. And if it gets stuck, ask Carol to help."

"Oh dear, Lord." Sarah breathed out.

Principal Wheeler cracked a smile. "She's not that bad once you get to know her."

"I think she's already made her mind up about me. There is no hope for us, I'm afraid." Sarah stood and gathered her purse and hat. "Oh, and where is my classroom?"

"Take a right out of the office and then take the second hallway to the left. Her room is at the end of the hallway. You'll see her name on the door."

"Okay, thanks. I'll go get these run off first."

"I'm the one who should thank you. We usually don't have this much trouble finding a sub, but with this flu going around, it put us in a bind. Oh and Sarah, if you think you'll enjoy subbing for us, I can start some paperwork to put you on our list. We use subs not just when teachers get sick, but when they need to be off for doctor's appointments or family issues."

Sarah smiled. "Thanks. I would appreciate that."

CHAPTER 20

*S*he headed out of the principal's office and made a beeline for the teacher's lounge. She opened the door and stepped inside. Three other teachers were standing around sipping on coffee and chatting. They stopped when they saw her.

"Hi, I'm Sarah Williams. I'm the sub for Mrs. Gainsworth." She smiled."

An olive-skinned woman who appeared to be in her early thirties with beautiful brown eyes walked over and held out her hand. She wore dark slacks with a pretty floral blouse. "Hi, I'm Amy. I'm one of the kindergarten teachers. And I have to say, I love your outfit."

Sarah smiled and shook the woman's hand. "Thanks. I didn't have any slacks, so I wore this."

"Wearing a skirt in the sixth grade is a bad idea." A much older white-haired woman with ice blue eyes stirred her coffee and shook her head. "That's when those boys start to notice girls and it gets them all riled up."

Amy snorted, shaking her head. "You'll have to forgive Nancy. She's the fifth grade science teacher, and she knows nothing about fashion."

"Clothes are worn to cover the body, not to show off what God gave you." Nancy scowled and then glanced down at her navy twinset. "Women should wear something respectable."

Sarah bristled under the woman's words, but masked her discomfort with a smile. "I'll remember that next time and wear a suit."

Amy let out a laugh and squeezed Sarah's arm. "I think I'm going to like you."

A petite twig of a woman with kind blue eyes and shoulder length sandy blonde hair walked over from the corner. She smiled and ducked her head. "Hello. I'm Martha. I'm the other kindergartner teacher. My classroom is across the hall from Amy." She spoke in a quiet voice. and Sarah knew she liked her immediately.

Sarah smiled and shook her hand. "Hi, Martha. I'm Sarah. Nice to meet you."

Martha ducked her head once again. "If you need anything, let me know. I know it might be a bit confusing here when you first arrive."

"Thank you. I need to run off some papers off before class starts." She held up her single paper.

"Yes, right over here." Amy walked over. She held out her hand. Sarah handed her the paper that needed to be copied.

Amy opened the lid of the printer, placing the paper in the correct position. "All you do is enter the number of copies you need," she looked at Sarah."

"I have forty-four kids total, but I'll need extra just in case."

"So we'll set it for fifty." Amy entered the number. "Now you hit black and white, and then start." Amy hit the last button. The machine rumbled to life, slowly spitting out copies.

"Thank you so much. I really appreciate it." Sarah smiled.

Amy went back to the table and grabbed her coffee. "And there's usually fresh coffee in the coffee pot. We've tried to get Carol to buy a keurig but she won't hear of it. But she keeps us in fresh coffee so I suppose that's all that matters."

"I would assume caffeine is essential to this job." Sarah grinned.

"Yes, you have no idea." Amy nodded.

The door opened and two more teachers walked in. They both stopped talking when they spotted Sarah.

"You must be the sub for Gainsworth." A tall lanky woman in her forties with short brown hair with matching eyes set her purse down on the table. "I'm Debbie. I teach sixth grade science."

"I'm Sarah. And yes, I'm the sub for Mrs. Gainsworth. Are our classrooms on the same hall?"

Debbie poured herself a cup of coffee and nodded. "Yes, they are. I'm two doors down from where you'll be today."

"Hi, I'm Milly. I teach English." A pretty blonde hair woman with blue eyes gave Sarah the once over. She appeared to be in her late thirties and wore dark designer jeans with a fashionable top. She even wore stylish nude espadrille.

"Hello. I'm Sarah." Sarah smiled.

Milly cocked her head. "You don't remember me, do you?"

"I'm afraid not." She frowned, trying to rack her brain. "I don't remember graduating with a Milly. The only Milly I remember was…"

"Was the girl who you stole the show from?" Milly finished her sentence.

The room went silent and Sarah could feel all eyes on her.

"What show, Milly?" Amy frowned. "I didn't know you were in a show?"

"It was when we were little. And it was a Christmas special. It was supposed to be my special at church. Until Sarah snatched the microphone away and started singing O' Holy Night."

Sarah let out an uncomfortable laugh. "That's not the way I remembered it."

"How do you remember it?" Nancy lifted her chin, looking ready to defend Milly.

"Well…"

Milly let out a laugh. "Let's let by gones, be by gones. That was a million years ago. Besides, everyone has moved on and it was silly kid stuff."

Sarah had a sinking feeling that Milly hadn't let

anything go. She'd known people like that who said one thing and did another. It was those kinds of people that she didn't let into her life.

"Great. Then let's get one last cup of coffee before the bell rings." Amy shook her head, and then looked at Sarah. "Are you a coffee drinker?"

"Absolutely. couldn't get through the day without it." Sarah walked over to the copier and pulled off her copies. She set them on the table, and then took the cup of coffee that Amy had so kindly offered. "Thank you."

"You're welcome. Sit. It may be the only time you get all day." Amy warned.

Sarah took a seat at the long table, took a sip of her coffee, and sent up a silent prayer that today would be a good day.

CHAPTER 21

Sarah had worked many jobs while she was traveling on the road. Her preferred job was, of course, singing in bars where the tips grew larger as the crowd grew bigger. When singing gigs were scarce, she worked as a server and a bartender. When she'd been desperate enough, she worked as a hotel maid during spring break week in Malibu, California. What a hotel full of out-of-town college students left behind had made her vow never to work in the hospitality industry again. It had turned her stomach.

But now, standing in the middle of her classroom, she knew sixth graders were definitely grosser than any college fraternity.

"Eww, gross." Mandy, who sat in the front row, grabbed her backpack and headed for the door.

"It looks like cheese." The kid named Mark cocked his head.

That sent another round of gags through the room.

Sarah ran over to open a window. She stuck her head out and sucked in a breath of fresh air.

"Miss Substitute?"

"It's Miss Williams," she reminded the class.

"Can we leave? It smelled like sour milk, and I have a weak stomach."

Sarah turned around and looked at the boy, who'd caused all the trouble to begin with.

"I don't think there's anything else left in your stomach, Marshal. I'm pretty sure all that milk you drunk at lunch for your TikTok challenge is all right there." She pointed to the white substance on the floor. "Who dared you to do that?" She glared at all the students in the room.

"No one. I needed more views on TikTok."

She rolled her eyes at the boy, who'd thrown up at least half a gallon of milk. She frowned. "I thought the cafeteria only let you have one carton of milk for lunch?"

He groaned and rubbed his stomach. "They do. But since everyone knew I was doing the TikTok challenge, everybody started giving me their milk."

"I've never seen someone throw up that much milk in my life." Todd shook his head and handed the iPhone back to Marshal. "I posted your video to TikTok."

Sarah marched over and snatched the phone out of Marshal's hand. "Give me that. You're not supposed to be using your phone during class time."

"How's he going to go viral if he can't have his phone?" Todd frowned.

"I don't feel so good." Marshal eased back into his desk and laid his head down.

Sarah tossed the phone on his desk.

"Miss Williams, I can't stay or I'm going to be sick." Mary held her shirt collar over her nose.

Sarah glanced at the time on the clock. "Okay it's almost time for school to be out. Everyone, go stand in the hall. Todd, you go get the janitor to clear this up."

"Me?" he whined.

"Yes, you." She glared at him.

He sighed heavily and then headed out the door to find the janitor. The other kids quickly filed out into the hallway.

Debbie, the teacher she'd met earlier, stuck her head in the room. "Sarah, why are all these kids standing in the hallway? They're being really loud and disruptive."

"I'm so sorry," Sarah walked over to her. "One kid got sick," she turned and pointed to the mess in the middle of the floor, "and the smell was making all the kids sick."

Debbie pulled a face and stepped back into the hallway. "I see. Does the janitor know?"

"Yes, I sent Todd to get him."

"Were they doing that TIktok challenge?"

"Yes." Sarah gritted out.

Debbie shook her head. "Why can't kids do normal things like pass notes in class?"

Sarah opened her mouth to respond, but spotted

Principal Wheeler heading in her direction. She poked her head in Sarah's classroom and wrinkled her nose. "And what is that smell?"

"Move out of the way, everyone," the janitor came barreling down the hallway, pushing a bucket and mop.

"One of the kids got sick." Sarah stepped aside to let Principal Wheeler inside. She pointed to the mess on the floor.

"Oh go.. "She slammed her hand over her mouth and backed out of the room.

"My stomach still hurts." Marshal leaned his head against the wall and wrapped his arms around his stomach.

"It should, dude. You almost drank and entire gallon of milk." Todd stated.

Principal Wheeler sighed. "Was this a Tiktok challenge?"

"Yes." Sarah rolled her eyes.

"Alright, all the kids go to the entrance and sit down against the wall. It's almost time for the bell, anyway. We need to get this room aired out. And Marshal, you go to my office. I'm calling your parents."

Marshal didn't have the energy to argue. The boy looked too green. The rest of the kids hurried to the entrance, and Amy went back into her classroom.

Sarah turned and looked at Principal Wheeler. "Honest to God, I thought I was going to make it through the day without an incident. So what if half the girls in my first class couldn't stop asking me questions about where I bought my clothes? So what if the next class was late arriving because of going over on time in music class, and none of the students finished their work? I even spent half of recess making sure the first graders weren't playing with that aggressive dog that wandered in into the playground. Thank God for Amy, who managed to chase it off before it bit someone. But this," she spread her hands out and looked over at the janitor cleaning up the mess, "This is how I end the day. On a vomit induced challenge."

Principal Wheeler patted her on the shoulder. "Be thankful that's all they were doing. You'll be surprised at some of the crazy things kids will do for social media." She nodded at Sarah. "Why don't you get Johnny and go home? I talked to Mrs. Gainsworth, and she said she's already feeling better. She should be back on Monday."

"Thank God," Sarah muttered.

Principal Wheeler grinned. "Teaching is not for everyone."

Sarah grabbed her purse along with her hat and looked the principal in the eye. "No, it is not. I applaud those who are great at it. You have my profound respect." She said her goodbyes and headed to Johnny's classroom to get her brother before heading home for what she hoped was a peaceful weekend.

CHAPTER 22

*S*arah had taken a long shower as soon as she got home to get rid of the memory of the day and the smell of sour milk.

She wrapped a towel around her hair and quickly dressed in cut-off denim shorts with a yellow T-shirt.

"Sarah! Uncle Oliver came back!" Johnny sprinted into her room, his face illuminated with joy.

"Oh, joy," she muttered. "I'll be down as soon as I dry my hair."

Johnny raced downstairs to see his favorite uncle.

Sarah picked up the hair dryer and turned it on. Her gut twisted as she dried her hair.

Her mind raced with intrusive thoughts.

Why was he back?

Where had he gone all week?

What did he want?

She set the hair dryer down on the bathroom

counter and slipped on her white sneakers. She could hear voices in the kitchen.

Uncle Oliver would probably expect dinner.

Shaking her head, she made her way to the kitchen.

Johnny and Uncle Oliver were sitting at the kitchen table looking over what appeared to be a photo album. Uncle Oliver looked up when she entered. "Hello, Sarah! Johnny was just telling me about your adventure being a substitute teacher. Heard some kid got sick in your class."

She forced a smile. "Hello, Uncle Oliver. Yes. Apparently he was doing some TIktok challenge." She nodded at the album. "What's that?"

"It's an old album I found when me and your mom were kids. I thought Johnny would like to see how close we were when we were little and how much trouble we used to get into." He glanced back down at the album. "And this is where we would go fishing during the summer."

She grabbed a glass out of the cabinet and filled it with water from the refrigerator. She leaned back against the counter and took a drink, keeping her gaze zeroed in on her uncle.

"But that looks like a pond." Johnny shook his head. "Do you know what's in a pond? Snakes, and alligators, and catfish the size of humans."

Uncle Oliver threw back his head and laughed. "We don't get many alligators here, and I'm not so sure about the catfish."

"But Johnny's right. There are snakes." Sarah crossed her arms over her chest.

"Well, we were just kids having fun. Back then we didn't have time to be scared about anything." Uncle Oliver smiled.

"So how come you weren't here when we got back from camping?" Sarah cocked her head.

"I had to take care of an issue with my business. Sorry, I didn't have time to cook. But I'm here now, and I'm going to make dinner tonight." Uncle Oliver stood and rubbed his hands together. "You both like steaks, right?" He walked over to the refrigerator and opened the freezer door.

"We don't have any steaks." Sarah cocked her head.

"Looks like you don't have much of anything." He frowned. "That's surprising. I guess you've not had a chance to run to the grocery."

"Actually, I went Tuesday." She lifted her chin.

"You can't survive on frozen pizza and chicken nuggets." He frowned as he dug around in the freezer.

"Miss Hannah brings us dinner." Johnny offered. "So we don't starve."

Sarah shot her brother a glare, but he was too busy looking at the old photos that he didn't notice.

"Miss Hannah must be a great friend." Uncle Oliver pulled out some chicken breasts.

"She's our neighbor." Johnny added.

"It's good to have neighbors that look out for you," Oliver held up a package of chicken breasts and some frozen veggies. "How about stir fry? All I need is some rice and a wok."

"it's in the pantry." Sarah opened the pantry door and retrieved the wok off the shelf. She glanced around, hoping her uncle wasn't going to give her a lecture on all the different kinds of cookies she had on hand. She retrieved the bag of rice and quickly shut the pantry door before he could investigate further into their eating habits.

"Perfect. Now, how about something to drink while I cook? I didn't see any beer in the refrigerator. How about some wine?" He gave her an expectant look.

"I don't have any wine."

"So you don't drink?"

"She drinks when she's with Miss Hannah and Miss Carolina." Johnny shut the album and slid off the chair. "Can I play my video games?" He looked up at her.

"Sure." She spoke without thinking.

Johnny race upstairs.

"Do you need any help?" She narrowed her eyes at him. Although she wasn't much of a cook, she didn't like the idea of him poking around in her kitchen.

"No worries. Now, you run along while I get every-thing prepped for dinner." He was already busy opening cabinets and pulling out seasonings.

Sarah didn't bother arguing. She needed some space away from him and grabbed her purse. Pullin out her cell phone, she headed out the back door into the back-yard. She walked until she got to the old tire swing in the back yard. Tossing her purse on the ground, she stuck her legs through the tire and sat.

She held out her phone, but her fingers hesitated over the contact list.

She could call Hannah, but she didn't want her to worry about her.

Carolina was a good choice, but she was still at work and she didn't want to bother her.

She spotted Noah's number and hit the call button.

It ran only once before he picked up.

"Noah Wellington. What can I do for you?"

"You can come get my sneaky uncle and take him away from here."

"So he's sneaky, huh?" A hint of amusement tinted his voice.

"Yeah, he is."

"What did he do, Sarah?"

"Nothing yet. But I'm sure he's up to something." She pushed her foot against the ground, setting the swing in motion. "He's actually in my kitchen right now. Cooking dinner."

"How criminal. Shall I call the police?"

"Noah, this is serious. You don't know him like I do."

"That's true."

"I'm sorry I called. I didn't mean to interrupt you at work."

"Not a problem. I was actually in between clients. How was your first day as a teacher?"

"Substitute teacher. And one kid threw up after

some Tiktok challenge. We had to evacuate the room because of the smell."

"Wow, I don't' know what to say to that."

"I can definitely say I won't be doing that again. Cross off that as a possible occupation."

"Sarah, you haven't said anything about singing. That's an occupation as well."

She sighed heavily. "Hopeton doesn't have a demand for singers."

"Maybe not, but what about song writing? I remember you writing songs in high school. Do you still do that?"

"Good memory."

"Thanks. I remember the things that matter."

His words made a smile play on her lips.

"well, haven't you written anything new?"

"I was working on something. But I haven't had time to finish it. Not since I've been looking for a job."

"So work on it this weekend. Get your guitar and sit out by the lake, or get in your van and take off for the woods. I'm sure your uncle wouldn't mind watching Johnny for a night while you get the creativity flowing."

"Your idea sounds lovely. But I can't leave Johnny with Uncle Oliver." She sighed heavily.

"What's the worst that can happen? Give the guy some credit. He was your mom's brother."

She grimaced. Noah was right. It wasn't like Oliver was going to run off with Johnny. Raising a kid wasn't Uncle Oliver's style.

"He might refuse." She stared out across the lake as

she longed to have a night away for herself to get some writing done.

"He might. But I doubt it. He's probably trying to make up for lost time between you two. He lost a sister, so he's probably feeling like he wants to get close to the family he has left."

She stopped swinging. "Maybe you're right."

"Just give him a chance. Besides, you need a night away. My parents have some land out in the country off Parker Road. It's about forty acres and has an apple orchard on it. There's even a fire ring. You can park your van. No one will bother you out there."

"Really? That sounds wonderful."

"Sure. I'll tell my parents you'll be out there and then text you the directions."

"Thanks, Noah." She already felt lighter.

"I'm here anytime you need me."

She hung up the phone and mentally prepared herself to ask her uncle for a favor.

CHAPTER 23

$\mathcal{S}$arah opened the door to her van and glanced around at her gorgeous surroundings. The apple orchards were alive with white blossoms on the brittle branches, and the fragrance was delightful.

She got out and walked over to the picnic table set up underneath the trees. There was a small basket with a box of chocolates and a note. She picked up the letter and opened it.

"Here's something sweet to help find your inspiration." ~Noah.

She smiled, opening the box of chocolates. Noah knew her penchant for junk food, and it was a sweet gesture.

She walked over to the fire ring and noticed Noah had already prepped the wood for a fire.

She'd have to do something thoughtful for him to return the favor of letting her come out to his parents' place.

She glanced at the time on her phone. Almost seven thirty. She still had some daylight to get some writing done.

She pulled out her guitar from the van and grabbed her notebook with the pen from her backpack.

She headed over to the picnic table to set them down.

Sarah glanced at her watch. Uncle Oliver had been more than happy to stay overnight with Johnny when she had asked him to babysit over dinner. Johnny was thrilled to have some alone time with his uncle, who promised to play catch with him in the backyard.

She hated to admit it. but maybe Noah was right. Maybe her uncle really was trying to reconnect with the only family he had left.

Sarah headed back to the van and pulled out a battery operated lantern, just in case she wrote long in to the night.

She sat down at the picnic table, shoved her hat on her head, and picked up her guitar. She strummed the tune, The Nearness Of You, by Norah Jones, one of her favorites, and slowly sang the lyrics.

The music seemed to float up and away on the gentle breeze of the spring evening. The scent of glossy green grass and apple blossoms surrounded her in a cozy, welcoming hug.

By the time she finished the song, a couple of birds had landed on the branches of the apple tree in front of her. The audience grew when a squirrel came down from the tree and stood at the base of the trunk, his tiny hands clasp together.

"Another?" She addressed her tiny crowd.

When none of the animals moved away, she launched into another song.

As she sang, her body filled with joy, and all the worries she'd been carrying for so long began to fall away, like autumn leaves.

The light faded into darkness. She stood, laid her guitar on the table, and stretched. Digging around in the basket, she found some matches. She went over to the fire ring and lit the kindling. The fire grew until flames danced upward to the darkening sky.

Sarah sat back down at the picnic table, picking up her pen and notebook. She turned the pages of her unfinished song.

"Sitting here, in my loneliness, thinking back over the past,

Reminded how much I lost when memories press down on me, making me downcast,

Now the summer of my heart is gone, leaving behind the winter of heartache,

My grief is still raw, after all this time, and I wonder, will live a life of heartbreak

"Or am I destined to live a life without pleasure or joy?

I want to cry until there's nothing left in me.

I want the pain to stop so I can breathe again

But your memory haunts the very depths of me

And I'm forever a prisoner of pain under lock and key.

As she wrote, her pen flew across the paper, while

tears ran down her face. She pulled the lantern closer so she could see as she scribbled down lyrics.

When the song was done, she started another with the same theme. Love and grief.

It was the hoot of an owl that finally broke her out of her writing sprint.

She set her pen down, yawned, and looked around. The fire had died down to just orange embers.

She pulled her phone out of the back pocket of her jeans. Two a.m.

She'd been writing nonstop for hours.

As she stood, she collected her guitar and notebook. Opening the side door of the van, she leaned her guitar against the wall by her bed. She changed into some shorts with a T-shirt and crawled on top of the bed. Reaching down, she opened the back of the van.

Crawling under the sheets, she looked out into the starry night sky, as she drifted off to sleep.

CHAPTER 24

*S*arah woke up to the sunlight streaming into her face. She blinked and slowly sat up.

"Sarah?"

She frowned and climbed out of the van from the back. She spotted Noah walking toward her down the tiny road she'd driven in on.

"Good morning." She called back.

"I hope you slept well." The closer he got, she realized he was holding two large Styrofoam cups. Tiny whiffs of steam came out from the tiny opening of the lids.

"Is that what I think it is?"

He stopped in front of her. "Coffee. I figured you were too busy to get out here last night that you forgot to pack any caffeine." He held one cup out to her.

"I could kiss you." She took the hot cup and lifted it to her lips. She took a sip and sighed at the heavenly taste.

"I wouldn't mind if you did." A small grin played on his lips.

She smiled as she looked at him. "Noah, can I ask you something?"

"Sure." He walked over to the picnic table to sit down.

She followed him and sat beside him. "Why haven't you remarried? Or at least found a girlfriend?"

He stared thoughtfully at his coffee. "Lots of reasons, I suppose. I have gone on dates. Some are better than others. But at the end of the date, there doesn't seem to be a ... "

"Spark?"

His eyes met hers. "Exactly. I keep waiting to see if the goodnight kiss results in a spark. You know, the kind you feel all the way to your toes. And when you get home you're still thinking about the kiss and the girl."

She studied the ground. Sadly, she couldn't relate. She'd never felt that way towards anyone. Her music always took precedence over relationships.

"And then there's being too busy. Raising Nathalie is a full-time job. As you know."

She took a sip and nodded. "I never knew how much it requires raising a child. And I don't mean monetarily." She studied him. "Do you think you'll ever get married again?"

"Honestly, I don't know. I mean, I would love to be married again, but it may not be in the cards for me." He looked at her. "What about you?"

"As you can see, I don't actively have any suitors breaking down the door asking for my hand in marriage."

"Not yet." Noah grinned.

She felt her face heat, and she took a quick sip of coffee. It was definitely time to change the subject. "Thanks to you and your parents for letting me stay here last night, I managed to finish a project or two."

"Really? Want to play it for me?" He gave her a hopeful look.

"Well, you brought me coffee. I suppose a song is the least I can do." She set her coffee down on the picnic table and headed for her van. When she came back, she had her guitar and notebook in hand.

She sat on the top of the table and began strumming. She started into the song she'd finished, which spoke of grief, loss and loneliness. Any feelings of embarrassment at what Noah would think quickly faded into the lyrics of the song.

When she was done, she opened her eyes and looked at him. He stared back at her with emotion in his eyes.

"Well? Aren't you going to say something?" She held her guitar tighter to her chest.

"Sarah. That was … beautiful."

The emotion in his eyes humbled her.

"Thank you." She studied the ground. "Once I started writing, I couldn't stop. I finished this song and wrote some others." She looked up at him. "I couldn't have done this if you hadn't arranged for this. Again, thank you."

A slow smiled stretched across his face. "I'll be here for you, supporting you and your dreams. I hope you know that."

She cocked her head. "You really mean that?"

"Of course, I do. Why wouldn't I?" He took a sip of coffee.

She shook her head. "It's not like my dreams are going to happen any time soon. I'm stuck here until Johnny graduates."

"You never know." Noah looked out across the countryside.

"Are you sure you liked the song? What about the chorus? I can't tell if it was high enough or if I should change the key."

Noah pulled out his phone. "I think it was great, but you are the expert. Why don't I film you while you sing it again? I'll text it to you. Then you can review and make changes."

She smiled. "You don't mind?"

"Of course not." He stood and pulled up the camera on his phone while she grabbed her guitar.

He looked at her. "Tell me when to record."

She took a deep breath, put her hat on her head, and nodded once before launching into the song she'd crafted.

CHAPTER 25

arah was home before ten that Saturday morning. She spotted Uncle Oliver's car in the driveway. Any reservations she'd had about her uncle were slowly slipping away.

She unlocked the front door and stepped inside. She placed her purse on the foyer table and headed into the kitchen.

Uncle Oliver was standing by the kitchen sink, sipping on a cup of coffee. "Sarah. I didn't expect you back so soon. Did you have a good time camping?"

"It was very productive," she smiled to herself and poured a cup of coffee.

"That's an odd way of describing sleeping out in a van." Uncle Oliver shrugged and put his coffee cup in the sink.

"How did everything go last night?"

He smiled. "Great. After we cleaned up the kitchen, we ended up watching movies."

"Really?" She expected Uncle Oliver was going to try to impress Johnny by taking him bowling or going for ice cream. "Is he awake?"

"Nah. We stayed up late. Little guy won't be up for another couple of hours." He picked up a stack of envelopes on the counter. "Oh, and I brought your mail inside."

She took them out of his hand and frowned. "Thanks. Exactly how late did you guys stay up?"

"I don't know. It was after midnight. He was having so much fun that we couldn't stop."

She took a sip of her coffee. "So, what are your plans? Staying another night?"

"I have to run over to Charlotte to check on a business opportunity. If I bought it, I could be closer to you guys." He smiled.

Noah's words came back to her. *He just wants to be closer to his family.*

"That would be nice, Uncle Oliver." She nodded, setting her cup down. "I'm going to grab a shower and chance clothes. Camping is wonderful, unless you don't have access to a shower."

Sarah walked upstairs to her room. She stopped at Johnny's room to peek her head inside.

Johnny was on his back, fast asleep. His mouth was slightly ajar, and his long lashes brushed the tops of his cheeks. His bedside lamp was still on, so she quietly stepped inside the room and turned it off. She pulled up the covers he'd kicked off during the night.

Something in her heart tugged at the sight of him. He looked so peaceful and even angelic.

After Sarah turned and headed to her room. She shut the door behind her, took off her clothes, and turned on the shower.

As the hot water washed over her, she closed her eyes and thought about the lyrics of the songs she had written.

By the time she got out of the shower, the water was lukewarm. She quickly dressed and dried her hair.

As she was slipping on her sneakers, she heard a timid knock on her door. She went and opened it.

"Johnny." She grinned. "I figured you would be asleep until lunch."

"Sorry I slept so long." He rubbed his eyes and yawned. "Did you enjoy your time away?"

She frowned. "I got a lot of song writing done. I slept in my van so that was nice. Are you hungry?"

He shook his head. "My stomach hurts."

She pressed her hand to his head. "You don't have a fever. Maybe you caught a stomach bug. Come downstairs and I'll get you something to help your stomach." She guided him down the stairs and into the kitchen.

"Where's Uncle Oliver?" Johnny whined.

"I'm not sure. Sit here." She pointed him to the chair at the kitchen table. She went to the front door and opened it. Uncle Oliver's car was gone.

She groaned. She shut the door before heading into the kitchen. "I guess he had to leave for work. But he said something about moving closer to Charlotte so he can see us. You'd like that wouldn't you?" She opened the cabinet to find the pink bottle of Pepto-Bismol.

She looked over at him.

Johnny stood up, grabbed his stomach ,and turned green. She dropped the bottle when she realized what was coming next.

She ran over, snatched him up and raced out the backdoor just as he got sick. She held onto him until he was finished being sick, and then knelt down to look at him.

"I'm sorry, Sarah." Johnny looked at her with tears in his eyes.

"You don't have to be sorry for anything. You can't help that you got sick. Besides, it was better to do it outside than on the kitchen floor." She smiled and wiped his tears away.

"I knew I shouldn't have eaten all those snacks, but Uncle Oliver said it was okay. I just got scared watching those movies, but Uncle Oliver kept telling me that's what big kids do. Eat snacks and watch movies" He wiped his face with the sleeve of his shirt. She tried not to cringe.

"Let's take your shirt off and get you in the shower. You'll feel better once you get cleaned up." She lead him back inside and upstairs to his bathroom. She turned the water on and helped him get undressed to his underwear.

She frowned and looked at him. "What snacks are you talking about?"

"The box of chocolate chips cookies and the Twinkies in the pantry," he sniffled.

"Johnny, you ate all of that?"

He nodded.

"And Uncle Oliver let you? Did he eat them with you?" She tried to keep her voice calm.

He shook his head. "No. He gave me the snacks and told me to watch the scary movies while he cleaned up in your room and Dad's office."

She jerked upright. "He went into my room?"

"Yes, he said he was going to straighten things up to make it look like a home. Then he put those awful movies on, and I got scared. I've never seen movies like that. I couldn't go to sleep with the lights off. So, I stayed up so late."

Dread grew in her stomach. It was one thing for Uncle Oliver to be snooping around in her room and her dad's office to steal something, but forcing Johnny to watch movies that were not appropriate for a child his age was quite another.

Sarah knelt down in front of him. "Do you know the names of the movies he made you watch?"

He shook his head. "It had a scary guy with a mask and a knife. He was going into people's houses and killing them."

"You're not going to watch those movies again, okay?"

"I'm sorry, Sarah." His bottom lip quivered.

"It's not your fault. It was Uncle Oliver's fault. He's

the adult. He should have known better." She pressed her lips into a thin line.

"Is Uncle Oliver in trouble?" Johnny looked up at her with fear in his eyes.

She gave him a smile. "Don't worry about Uncle Oliver. I want you to get a shower to get cleaned up. Then come downstairs and I'll get you some ginger ale and medicine. It will make you feel better, okay?"

"Okay." He nodded, and she left him alone to get cleaned up.

Anger burned inside her veins so hot, she wanted nothing more than to wring Uncle Oliver's neck.

She decided if he ever came back, she was going to make it perfectly clear he was not welcome in their home or their lives.

CHAPTER 26

"*I* can't believe he did that." Sarah stopped pacing in her backyard, turning to look at Noah. She'd called him after getting Johnny cleaned up. She'd given him some medicine along with a ginger ale. He was currently resting on the couch watching classic cartons.

"Maybe he was just spoiling him for the night." Noah grimaced.

"No. I'm not buying it. He's the adult. Besides, would your parents ever let Nathalie eat that many snacks while they are baby-sitting her?"

Noah let out an enormous sigh. "No. They wouldn't."

"That's because they love her."

"I'm sure your uncle loves Johnny and you, too."

She propped her hands on her hips. "I wish you would stop defending him."

He stood up from the Adirondack chair and gently

grabbed her arms. "Sarah, I'm not defending him. I'm just trying to see the other side."

She lifted her chin, stepping out of his grip, and turned to stare out across the lake. "Let's just change the subject. The more we talk, the angrier I get thinking about it."

"Sarah…"

She spun to face him. "Hannah called. She said that the post office is hiring. Of course, I'll have to pass some tests to qualify."

He frowned. "What kind of position? Would you be a mail carrier?"

She shook her head. "No. I would start out sorting the mail in the back. With some time and experience, they could be promoted to working the window. Pay is decent, and it has wonderful benefits and a great retirement."

Noah frowned "Being stuck inside all day sorting mail doesn't really sound like a job you would enjoy."

"I have to pay the bills, Noah. I don't have the luxury of doing what I want"

He cocked his head and opened his mouth, like he wanted to say more.

She was in no mood to listen. "Thanks for coming over. I'm sorry to take you away from Nathalie on your Sunday afternoon."

"Not a problem. I'm glad you called.' He stepped closer.

"I need to get back inside and check on Johnny."

He nodded and made his way over to the gate that led out of the backyard to the driveway.

She hurried up the steps and opened the back door. Quickly she stepped inside the kitchen. There was the faint noise of cartoons playing in the living room.

Sarah peeked her head around the corner. Johnny was sitting up, clutching the pillow to his chest. He glanced over at her.

"How are you feeling?"

"Better."

"Feel like eating some soup? I have some chicken noodle."

He nodded and looked back at the TV.

She smiled and headed into the kitchen. There was a can of chicken noodle soup and some crackers in the pantry. After grabbing a pot, she poured in the contents of the soup.

While the soup was warming, she opened up the box of crackers and placed some on a plate.

Pulling down a bowl from the cabinet, she poured in the hot soup and placed it on the plate with the crackers.

She retrieved a cold ginger ale out of the refrigerator and popped the top. She put everything on a tray and carried it to the living room.

"Here we go." She set the tray down on the coffee table.

Johnny slid off the couch to sit on the floor. She sat down in the chair and watched as he ate.

"Tomorrow is your book report. Have you finished it?"

He nodded without looking at her.

"I need to read over it when you get done."

He rolled his eyes.

She smiled. He was definitely feeling better.

Her phone rang.

Sarah got up and pulled the phone out of her jeans pocket. "Hi Carolina. I wasn't expecting to hear from you."

"Sarah, are you at home?" There was an urgency in the woman's tone.

"I am. Why? Is something wrong?"

Carolina hesitated. "I'm not sure. I just had a visit from Child Protective Services"

"That's weird. I thought you didn't have any children."

"I don't. She wasn't here to talk about me. She were here asking questions about you. I have a feeling they are on their way to your house."

"Me?" Sarah frowned. Just then, the doorbell rang.

"Sarah? Is everything okay?" Carolina asked.

"I don't know. That was the doorbell. I'll have to call you back." She hung up and walked to the front door.

She peered through the glass and saw an older woman in a pantsuit. Slowly, she opened the door.

"Can I help you?" she asked.

"Are you Sarah Williams?" The woman shoved her glasses up on the bridge of her thin nose and peered at Sarah. She had pulled her mousy brown hair into a tight bun at the back of her neck, and the only makeup she wore was bright red lipstick, which only accentuated her pale white skin.

"Yes."

"I'm Miriam Hadley, and I'm with Child protective services. We've had a report concerning Johnny Williams. I'm here to do a home visit to make sure he's not in any immediate danger."

"Danger?" She gave the woman an incredulous look.

"Can I come in or shall I call the police to let me in the residence?"

Shocked and confused, Sarah stood there for a minute trying to comprehend the woman's words.

"Miss Williams?" Miriam pulled out her cell phone.

"No. You can come in. Johnny's in the living room." Sarah stood to the side to allow Mrs. Hadley entrance to her home.

Dread filled every bone in her body. She shook her head. Surely this whole thing was a big mistake.

But as she knew, mistakes always came at a price.

CHAPTER 27

*S*arah sat on the couch beside Johnny as Mrs. Hadley asked her a barrage of questions.

"And is it true you've had your electricity cut off?" She held her pen at the ready, over the legal pad she'd been scribbling on every time Sarah answered a question.

"Yes, but it was…"

Before Sarah could explain, Mrs. Hadley was writing furiously on her notepad.

"You didn't let me explain."

"There's no need. These are merely yes or no questions."

"I hardly see how that's fair." Sarah glared.

Mrs.Hadley stared at her for a second and then went back to writing something else down.

"They cut my electricity off because I didn't get a bill for three months. I went down to the electric company and they straightened it out. It's on automatic withdrawal now." Sarah lifted her chin.

"Is it true that Johnny's lunch bill at school was late getting paid?" Mrs. Hadley cocked her head.

"Yes, but I never got a note saying it was due to be paid." Sarah glanced over at Johnny as he was engrossed in his cartoons.

"Miss Williams, the school said they not only sent out a letter in his backpack, but they also sent it out in an email."

"The school?" Sarah's eyes widened. "You've been speaking to the school?"

"I'm not allowed to speak about this case with you at the moment. I'm just gathering evidence." She looked down at her notepad and scribbled.

"I didn't get the email because they were sending it to my mother's email."

Mrs. Hadley didn't look up from writing. "How is Johnny's nutrition?"

"Nutrition?"

"Yes. Does he get regular home cooked meal, not including frozen pizza or mac and cheese."

Sarah narrowed her eyes. "Mrs. Hadley, I'm not sure why you are even here. Per my parent's wishes laid out in their will, I am Johnny's legal guardian. I need to know why you are here."

She looked up and shoved her glasses back up on the bridge of her nose. "Whenever there is a concern about a child's safety, CPS will send out someone to investigate. That's what I'm doing. I'm investigating."

"So someone called CPS on me." Her mouth dropped. "Was it Carol at the school?"

Mrs. Hadley cocked her head. "Interesting. Why would you think it was the school secretary?"

Sarah huffed. "Because she clearly hates me."

"She seemed pleasant enough when I spoke with her."

Sarah narrowed her eyes. "So it was her."

"Miss Williams, is it true that under your care a child got sick at school, and the room had to be evacuated?"

Sarah pressed her lips into a thin line. "I had nothing to do with that. I was substituting for the sixth grade and one kid did a Tiktok dare that made him get sick."

Mrs. Hadley scribbled.

Sarah rolled her eyes. "Look, if you can't tell me who called, can you tell me how I can clear this up?"

"Miss Williams, do you keep alcohol in the house?"

"No. I do not." She said defiantly.

"Is it true you often drink with neighbors while in the presence of Johnny?"

"It was one glass of wine, and it was at a dinner party." Her heart jackhammered in her chest.

Mrs. Hadley looked up. "You're not employed at the moment, are you?"

"I'm looking. I actually am going to the post office tomorrow to fill out an application."

"Have you worked in the postal service before?"

"No."

"What's your normal area of occupation?"

Sarah bit her lip. Never in her life had she been ashamed to say she was a singer/songwriter. But now, staring at Mrs. Hadley, a deep sense of unworthiness filled her soul.

She cleared her throat. "I'm a songwriter and singer."

Mrs. Hadley's eyebrows shot up. "Oh, have you written anything I might have heard?"

Sarah's shoulders slumped. "No, my plan was to go to Los Angeles to try to get a contract when my parents died. Instead, I came back here to raise my little brother."

"So you don't have a career at the moment?" Mrs. Hadley looked up.

"Like I said, I'm applying at the post office tomorrow." Sarah forced a smile.

"I'd like to ask Johnny some questions, if you don't mind."

"Of course. You can ask him anything." She swallowed hard.

"I'd like to speak to him alone." Mrs. Hadley lifted her chin.

Sarah's stomach dropped. She pasted on a confident smile and stood. "I'll just be in the backyard if you need me."

She walked through the kitchen. When she reached the back door, she strained to hear what was being spoken, but she couldn't hear a word.

She grabbed her phone out of her back pocket and headed outside.

Sarah paced around the yard and kept checking the time on her phone.

"Twenty minutes. What could they possibly be talking about for twenty minutes?" she muttered to herself.

She thought about calling Noah to let him know what was going on, but after their conversation earlier, she didn't want to feel like a burden to him.

Besides, she didn't want to keep relying on him.

"Miss Williams?"

Sarah spun around at the sound of Mrs. Hadley's voice.

"Yes?"

"A word, please." Mrs. Hadley disappeared into the house.

Sarah's throat was dry. As she made her way toward the house, the worst-case scenario played in her head.

When she closed the back door behind her, it barely registered a sound. It was almost like her ears were being drown out by white noise filling her mind.

She walked into the living room and realized Johnny wasn't there. Fear welled up inside of her.

"Where's my brother?" She looked at Mrs. Hadley.

"I asked him to go upstairs while I speak with you." Mrs. Hadley took her seat in the chair.

Sarah forced her feet to move across the living room floor. When she got to the couch, she had to remind herself to sit.

"Miss Williams. As per procedures, whenever we get a call about a possible endangered child we also have to do an investigation."

"Endangered child?" The words didn't even compute in her head. "What does that mean?"

"A child that is not getting the care and safe environment that he needs to thrive." Mrs. Hadley shoved her glasses up on the bridge of her nose.

"But Johnny is in a safe environment."

"That's up to me to decide." She glanced down at her notes. "Both parents are deceased, correct?"

"Yes, our parents died in a plane crash." She swallowed back the bitter lump in her throat.

"Are there any more living relatives? If not, then we are required to remove Johnny from the house and put him in foster care.

"Foster care?" She jumped from her seat.

"It would only be temporary." Mrs. Hadley assured her. "Unless there is another living relative…"

She couldn't let Johnny be placed in foster care. He was too fragile. He would be terrified.

"We have an uncle. Uncle Oliver." She blurted out.

"And does this uncle have employment?" Mrs. Hadley cocked her head.

"He's a successful business owner. He was just here this morning, visiting. If I call him, he will come back to stay with Johnny until this is all cleared up." She was glad she'd gotten Uncle Oliver's phone number before he left.

"Very well. But I must insist on staying here until he

shows up. If he agrees to stay in the house until our investigation is complete, then Johnny can remain in the house."

Sarah breathed out a sigh of relief. "Thank you."

Mrs. Hadley stood. She clasped her notepad to her chest and gave Sarah a once over. "You know, you are very young to be taking care of a child. No one will blame you if you decide to sign over custody of your brother to your uncle."

Sarah bit her lip to keep from telling the woman what she could do with her opinion. Instead, she pasted a smile on her face and excused herself to call her uncle, and prayed for a miracle.

hankfully, Uncle Oliver answered on the second ring. After Sarah gave him the rundown of what was happening, he quickly agreed to come back and stay with them until they straightened out the situation.

Mrs. Hadley had finally left after speaking with her uncle who agreed to come and stay with Johnny.

It was dark and she'd just gotten Johnny into bed. Johnny had a lot of questions about why Mrs. Hadley was there. Sarah had tried to downplay her visit as something routine and not anything he should worry about.

Now, standing outside in the backyard looking at the lake, Sarah felt like a failure. Maybe Mrs. Hadley was right. She was too young to be taking on the responsibility of raising Johnny.

"Sarah?"

She turned at the sound of her uncle's voice.

He gave her a sympathetic smile as he walked towards her. "Look, I'm glad you called. I know we haven't always been close…"

"Thanks for coming." She wrapped her arms around herself and stared at the ground. "I'm not sure what to do now. I know you can't stay here forever."

"Actually, I can."

She jerked her head up. "But what about your business?"

"I have been getting offers to sell my business. I could do that and stay here. That way I could see that Johnny gets the care he needs."

His words crawled over her skin. Was he insinuating that she couldn't take care of her brother?

She shook her head and tried to shove her suspicious thoughts away.

"I'm sure after this is cleared up, you can go."

"Sarah, I talked with Mrs. Hadley." His words were slow and measured. "There's no clearing this up."

"What do you mean?" Her stomach dropped.

"She said it would be better for me to take on the role of his legal guardian. Otherwise, they are going to put him in foster care."

"What? They can't do that." Her breathing grew faster.

"They are a government run system. They can do whatever they want." He gave her a sad look.

Her head swam, and purple stars danced before her eyes.

"Are you okay?"

"I need to sit down." She stumbled over to the Adirondack chair and sat. She rested her face between her hands, trying to control her breathing.

"He can't go into foster care. He just can't."

Her uncle knelt beside her and rested his hand on her shoulder. "Just calm down. Everything will be okay. Just keep your head."

She looked up at him. She had to do the right thing. As much as she didn't like her uncle, she couldn't bear to think of her brother being taken away from his home.

"If you become his legal guardian, will you promise to stay in Hopeton?" her throat hurt as she spoke.

"Of course. But we would have to do everything legally."

"I know." Her voice was soft.

'Why don't we go turn in for the night. You've had a rough day and you could use the sleep. We'll go see an attorney in the morning and talk about how to proceed."

She nodded. She didn't even have the energy to speak.

CHAPTER 29

*S*arah woke up at six the next morning. She sat up, yawned, and threw the covers off. She'd had a hard time falling asleep. When she finally drifted off, she had nightmares.

She pulled on some shorts under her T-shirt and padded downstairs to get some coffee.

Sarah stopped in her tracks when she spotted Uncle Oliver standing in the kitchen. He smiled when he saw her.

"Good morning, Sarah. I made coffee."

"Perfect," she mumbled, went to the cabinet and pulled down a mug. She fixed a cup of coffee and then sat down at the kitchen table to doctor it with cream and sugar.

"I need to go wake up Johnny."

"No need. I already did. He should be down in a minute." Uncle Oliver grabbed a skillet and put in on the stove. "I'm going to make grilled cheese for breakfast. Want me to make you one too?"

"No thanks."

"Not much of a breakfast eater? I get it." He hummed to himself as he coated the skillet with butter and then began making the sandwiches.

She grimaced at the noise he was making. Couldn't he just cook without all the singing?

She stood up just as Johnny came into the kitchen.

"Good morning." She smiled at him.

He gave her an odd look. "Why does your face look like that?"

"Like what?"

"Red and puffy." He slid into the chair, taking the glass of milk that Uncle Oliver put in front of him.

"Not enough sleep, I guess." Or that she'd cried herself to sleep. "Uncle Oliver is making grilled cheese sandwiches. Isn't that great?"

"I guess." Johnny took a sip of his milk.

"Are you feeling better today?" She lowered her voice.

He nodded as he wiped his mouth with the back of his hand. She smiled and plucked a napkin out of its holder to wipe his face.

"After you eat, your sister and I will take you to school."

She looked up at him and frowned. "We will?"

"Yes. I figured we could head over to the attorney's office this morning and get the legal paperwork started."

She shook her head. "But I have to go by the post office this morning to fill out an application"

He frowned. "Why? You won't need to get a job in Hopeton now. Not if I'm … "

Sarah stood up from her chair and shook her head. "Do you mind giving me and Johnny some privacy? I need to talk to him."

"But the grilled cheese." He flipped the sandwich.

"It's fine. I'll finish it." She held out her hand, and he put the spatula in her palm.

"I'll grab a shower." He headed out of the kitchen, giving them privacy.

"Why is Uncle Oliver back? I thought he had to go back to work?"

She flipped the grilled cheese and focused on the sandwich.

"He's going to be here for a while. To help take care of you." She swallowed the lump in her throat.

"Why? I don't need two people taking care of me."

She blinked back the sting of tears. "Johnny, sometimes we think we are ready for something and then when we have to rise to the occasion, we just can't do it."

"Like baiting a hook?" He looked at her.

"Not exactly." She pressed the spatula against the bread. The butter sizzled.

"Some people think that Uncle Oliver is a better person to take care of you."

"Is that why that woman was here yesterday, asking so many questions? The one that looked like a witch?"

She glanced over at him. He was staring at her.

"Yes. That's why she was here."

"I think you can take care of me. I don't need Uncle Oliver here." Johnny frowned.

"I'm only doing what's best for you. Sometimes making the right decision is hard."

She grabbed a plate, placing the grilled cheese sandwich on it. She walked over and set it down in front of her brother.

"I'm not hungry." He shoved his chair back and headed upstairs to his room.

She stared down at the plate. The grilled cheese sandwich was perfectly brown.

Sarah had finally not burned a meal.

CHAPTER 30

*A*fter dropping Johnny off at school, Uncle Oliver drove them over to the attorney's office. Mr. Willard was the attorney who Sarah's parents had used to draw up their will and set up the trust for the inheritance.

"I don't know that we can just walk in. We should make an appointment." She glanced nervously out the window of his car.

"I'm sure he'll be more than happy to see us since this is an emergency." Her uncle reassure her as he pulled into the parking lot. He killed the engine and climbed out of the car.

Stunned, she quickly gathered her wits about her and followed him to the door.

After stepping inside, they were greeted by the secretary. "Hello, how may I help you?"

"Hi. I'm Sarah Williams. I am…"

"Oh yes, Sarah. I remember you. Do you have an

appointment with Mr. Williard?" The older secretary named Mary frowned, looking down at her appointment book. "I don't have you down."

"I know. It's kind of an emergency. Something has happened that I need to see Mr. Williard about."

Mary's eyebrows shot up, and she reached for the phone. "Of course. Have a seat. I'll let him know you are here."

"Thank you." Sarah moved to a leather chair in the waiting room and sat. She clasped her trembling hands in her lap, trying to calm her racing thoughts.

"Miss Williams? Mr. Willard said you can go on back." Mary gave her a concerned smile and then cut her eyes at her uncle.

"Thank you." Her own words sounded hollow in her ears. She got up off the chair and walk down the hallway to Mr. Willard's office.

Since his door was open, she poked her head inside. "Hello Mr. Willard."

"Sarah." He stood and smiled. "Please come on in."

She stepped inside and clasped her hands in her lap. "Mr. Willard. Sorry for barging in like this, but this is important."

"Of course. Please sit down."

She took a seat, and her uncle sat in the chair beside her.

"This is my Uncle Oliver."

"Nice to meet you, Oliver," Mr. Willard held out his hand, and they shook.

"Now, tell me, what I can do for you, Sarah?" The

attorney placed his hands on the large mahogany desk and gave her his full attention.

She cleared her throat. "I'm here to see about signing over guardianship to my uncle."

Mr. Willard blinked. "I don't understand."

She opened her mouth, but Oliver spoke up. "Sarah realizes it's too much work for her to raise a young boy, so I have offered to take over his guardianship."

She bristled under his words and shot him a glare. "That's not exactly it."

Mr. Willard looked at them, sitting back in the chair. "Paperwork takes time. It's a tedious procedure."

"We were hoping to get this done quickly." Oliver stated with a fake smile.

"If you don't mind, may I have a word with Miss Williams?" Mr. Willard looked at her uncle.

"I don't see…"

"If you want the paperwork started today, then I will have to speak with my client privately." Mr. Willard pressed a button on his phone. Mary picked up. "Mary, can you come and get Mr. Williams to take him to the break room? He is in need of some of your homemade scones and coffee."

Within a few seconds, Mary appeared at the door. Olivier looked like he wanted to argue. But seemed to think better of it and followed Mary out of the door.

Mr. Willard stood up, walked around the desk, and shut the door before taking his seat.

"Sarah, what is this about?" He narrowed his eyes in concern.

"It's just…" The words burned her tongue and she couldn't seem to spit them out. She placed her hands on the desk and cleared her throat.

He reached across the desk and squeezed her hand. "Being a parent is not easy. But you've done a wonderful job since your parent's death."

She snorted. "Tell that to the CPS officer that visited my house."

Mr. Willard's eyes widened. "When did this happen?"

"Yesterday." She felt the hot tears free fall down her cheeks. "Someone made a complaint. Said I had the electricity cut off because I didn't pay my bill. They said they knew Johnny had a lunch debt that had been overdue and how I had financial difficulties. She says, I am too young to care for him. They threatened to put him in foster care if I didn't have a living relative that could stay with him until the investigation was over."

"I see." Mr. Williard handed her a Kleenex from the box sitting on his desk and narrowed his eyes. "Oliver is your mother's brother, correct?"

"Yes," she nodded.

"She and your father made their wishes perfectly clear that they wanted you as Johnny's guardian."

"I know. And I failed."

They sat there in silence for a while until Mr. Willard picked up the phone. "Please bring Oliver back in here."

Oliver stepped back inside the room with a smile.

"You were right, Mr. Willard, they were the best scones I've ever tasted."

Mr. Willard smiled. "Mary bakes them for Mondays. Says they help start the week off right." He clicked his keyboard. "Let me pull up the details of Johnny's Guardianship."

Sarah felt her heart drop. She couldn't believe after all she'd done, she was going to lose her brother.

Sure, they hadn't been close, and she'd been too busy traveling to visit often. But since her parents died, she'd given up her life to come back to Hopeton to do the right thing.

And she'd failed.

CHAPTER 31

"Okay, per your parents' wishes, they wanted Sarah to have guardianship over Johnny until his eighteenth birthday. Which means, you have insight into the inheritance your parents left him."

"I know." She mumbled..

"Would you like to share that with Olivier?" Mr. Willard urged.

"Johnny won't get his inheritance until he's eighteen years old." She paused. "He'll only get a portion of his inheritance when he's eighteen years old. Then he'll get another portion at twenty-one, and then again at age twenty-eight." She glanced over at Oliver.

His expression changed. "What? He doesn't get it now? How do the bills get paid?"

"I pay them." She frowned.

He jerked his head in her direction. "You don't even have a job."

"I was using the money I had saved up while traveling. That money's almost gone. That's why I was trying to get a job." She shook her head. "Why are you so worried about that, anyway? You don't have to worry about money."

"I'll continue reading the details of Johnny's guardianship, if you don't mind." Mr. Willard looked back at his computer. "In addition to supporting Johnny until he's eighteen, he's not allowed to move from Hopeton or the house. Since the house is paid for, he is to be cared for in his childhood home until the age of eighteen."

Uncle Oliver shook his head. "But I can't stay here." His eyes widened.

Sarah glared at him. "You told me earlier that you were selling your business and were moving to Hopeton to raise Johnny. Why are you changing your tune now?"

Her uncle's face went red, and he pressed his lips into a thin white line.

Realization settled in her chest.

"Mr. Willard, is there a room where my uncle and I can speak privately?" She didn't take her eyes off Uncle Oliver while she spoke.

"Sarah, why don't you two speak here? I'll step out. I have a matter I need to discuss with Mary, anyway." He got up from behind his desk and walked out, closing the door behind him.

Oliver stood up and walked over to the window. "What were your parents thinking? Not giving Johnny any money until he turns eighteen."

"They were making sure whoever was his guardian had his best interests at heart." Sarah stood as anger coursed through her veins. "I was right about you all along. You didn't come back because we were family. You came back to get something. Like you always do."

Her uncle shoved his hand through his hair. "This isn't how it was supposed to go. We were both supposed to get what we wanted out of this."

She crossed her arms over her chest. "And what exactly was that?"

"I was going to get my debts paid back to the loan shark that I owe, and you were going to go back to living in your van and doing whatever it is you do."

She slammed her eyes shut. "I should have listened to my intuition when you first showed up. If I had, you would have never been allowed inside my house."

She had been right about him all along.

"It's my sister's house." He turned around, narrowing his beady eyes at her.

"Not any more. It belongs to me and my brother." She studied him and then it hit her like a ton of bricks.

The unexpected visit. The offer to get to know Johnny.

"You were the one who called CPS."

When he said nothing, she pressed for an answer. "Uncle Oliver, answer me."

He spun around and glared. "I needed you out of the way, so I could get to Johnny's money. Before my sister died, I went to her to ask her for a loan. She almost agreed, but your dad butted in and refused to loan me anything. Do you know how much trouble I'm in with my gambling debt? There are men that will kill me if I don't pay it back."

Anger welled up in her with each word he uttered.

"So after they died, I figured they would have left everything to you and Johnny. I knew you didn't care for me, but Johnny did. Besides, it wasn't like I was going to take all of his inheritance. I just needed enough to pay my debt. I knew you wouldn't just hand over guardianship, so I had to force your hand. That's why I asked his teacher to email me and keep me updated."

"So you knew about the lunch debt before me?"

He nodded. " I found out when your electric bill was mailed out and made sure to take it out of your mailbox before you could see it. "

"You are the reason our electricity was cut off." Her mouth dropped. "What about me getting fired from Stanley's garage?"

"Who?" He frowned.

"Never mind." She shook her head. "Do you know they are still going to put Johnny in foster care? All because of a lie that you started?" She curled her fingers into fists. "I can't believe you would do this."

He swallowed hard. "My back was up against the wall. We are talking about my life here."

"No. We are talking about my brother's life, you idiot." She shouted.

Oliver took a step back. "I'm sorry. I didn't mean for

any of this to happen this way. It's just that I need money."

"How much money do you owe?"

"Two hundred thousand dollars."

Her legs went weak as she grabbed the desk for support. "You have got to be kidding."

"I wouldn't kid about this. What am I going to do?"

She eased into the chair. Her stomach dropped. She knew what she had to do. "You can start by calling CPS and telling them you lied about me being unable to care for my brother."

"But I'll get in trouble."

"I don't care!" She shouted.

The door opened slowly and Mr.. Willard poked his head in. "Is everything okay here?"

"No. It's not. Mr. Willard, please come in. I believe I need some attorney council."

"How may I be of service to you?" Mr. Willard gave her a smile.

"It seems that the circumstances have changed." She cut her eyes at her uncle. "It seems that there has been some light shone on why CPS was called."

"I see." Mr. Willard narrowed his eyes at Oliver. "How may I help clear up the confusion?"

"I want you to draft up a contract for my uncle to sign. He's going to make a written confession to CPS, saying he falsified the report of Johnny being endangered. He's going to confess to stealing my electric bill out of the mailbox."

"That's a federal offence." Mr. Willard glared.

Uncle Oliver squirmed in his seat.

"Yes. And that's why he's going to confess to Mrs. Hadley."

"Are you crazy? If I do that, then I'll go to jail." His eyes widened.

"There's something in it for you."

"I highly doubt that." He stood, went over to the window and looked out. He propped his hands on his hips.

"In exchange for telling the truth, I'm going to give you my inheritance."

Uncle Oliver spun around. Mr. Willard jumped out of his seat. "Sarah, you can't do that. It's all the money your parents left you."

"I know." Sarah said softly. "But if it will keep Johnny back under my guardianship, and get Oliver out of our life, then it's worth it."

Oliver opened his mouth to speak but couldn't find the words.

"How soon can you type up the agreement?" She looked at Mr. Willard.

"I'll keep it brief, so only a few minutes. In the meantime, Mr. Williams needs to call and confess to Mrs. Hadley at CPS."

"Yes, he does." She looked at her uncle.

Uncle Oliver slowly nodded. "I'll do it."

"Great. Now, if you two will excuse me, I have to go over to the post office to put in my application. I'll be back soon." She narrowed her eyes on her uncle. "I'm taking your car in case you change your mind. And if you leave before calling or signing that contract, then you won't get a dime out of me. Understood?" She held out her hands for his keys.

He lifted his cool eyes to her and simply nodded once as he handed her the keys.

She left the office and walked down the hallway to the front door.

"Sarah," Mr. Willard followed her.

She turned right before opening the door.

"You don't have to do this. I can call the authorities and have him arrested for what's he's done. And you can keep your money."

"And if you do that, then CPS will still do an investigation, and Johnny will have to go to foster care while it's being sorted out." She shook her head. "I won't do that to him. I just want Uncle Oliver out of our lives forever. This just gives me insurance that we won't see him again. Just have the paperwork ready for me to sign. I'll go by the bank to get the money after I put my application in." Sarah walked out the door and slid into Oliver's car. Then and drove to the bank and her interview.

CHAPTER 32

Sarah looked at her reflection in the mirror, and then cringed. The uniform wasn't her style, but at least she had a stable job. The past few weeks had been a blur. After leaving Mr. Willard's office, she put in her application and got an interview at the post office the same day. They were short staffed and needed someone who could start immediately. She started the next day.

When she got back to Mr. Willard's office, her uncle had signed the paperwork where he confessed to lying to CPS. Mr. Willards also assured her that he was present while Oliver called and talked to Mrs. Hadley. According to her attorney, Mrs. Hadley had given him an earful about the consequences of lying to a state agency.

"Sarah, where's my book?" Johnny called downstairs.

She smiled and shook her head. "Check under your covers. You were reading it before bed, remember?"

"Oh, yeah."

She heard his footsteps run up the stairs into his room. She turned around, and he was staring at her.

"What? You don't like the outfit?"

He shrugged. "It's better than what they make you wear at Burger King." He darted back downstairs.

She laughed, gathered her purse, and followed him.

Sarah stepped into the kitchen and found Johnny sitting at the kitchen table. He'd already set out two bowls and two spoons. He'd placed the box of Fruity Pebbles on the table and even gotten the milk out of the refrigerator.

"You did all this?"

"Yeah. I figured since it's just us we have to take care of each other." He poured the cereal into his bowl, and then almost over poured the milk.

She blinked back tears at his words. Struggling to contain her emotions, she poured herself a cup of coffee and sat down.

"Are you sad that it's just us? Do you miss Uncle Oliver?" She braced for his reaction.

"Not really. He was always talking and never listened to me when I had something to say. He's not like you. You listen to me." He shoved a spoonful of cereal into his mouth and chewed.

"I don't think he's going to be coming back. I think he's too busy with his job." She lied.

"He always gave me a funny feeling. I was just nice to him because I thought you liked him."

"Me?" She shook her head. "No. He gave me a weird vibe, too. I think it's best that it's just us from here on out." She sipped her coffee.

He shoved her cereal bowl towards her. "You need to eat before you go to work."

She smiled and dug her spoon into the bowl. "Yes, sir."

"Can Ben still come over after school?" He looked at her expectantly.

"As long as you two play outside. I think we can talk Carolina into letting Phoenix come over so you guys can play with him. How does that sound?"

His face lit up. "Great!"

She was grateful that Johnny had made her eat breakfast that morning. Once she got to work, she'd been so busy, she didn't get to eat lunch until one o'clock.

The work was monotonous, and she quickly got the hang of it.

It wasn't as exciting as singing, but it was a steady job with a paycheck. Both things she needed desperately.

The weeks flew by. School would be out for summer break in less than a week, and Sarah still didn't have a plan of what to do with Johnny while she worked.

Hannah would be out of town for the first two weeks of summer break to see her children. She offered to take Johnny with her, but Sarah said no. She didn't think she could bear to be away from him for that long. Carolina had said she could bring Johnny to work with her, but Johnny didn't want to go. He said Bertha scared him too much.

Sarah didn't argue. Bertha scared everyone.

That Friday night, she was cutting up some vegetables for dinner when her phone rang.

She picked it up.

Noah.

She smiled. "Hello?"

"Hey. Hope I haven't caught you at a bad time."

"Just cutting up vegetables for chicken pot pie."

"Sounds yummy. It looks like you have gotten this cooking thing down."

"It's one of Hannah's recipes. And yes, I 'm getting better at cooking. You and Nathalie want to come over for dinner so I can prove my cooking prowess?"

"Is that an invitation? Because I never turn down food."

"Yes."

"Then we'll be there around six. See you then." Noah ended the call.

She set her phone down and reached for two more plates out of the cabinet.

CHAPTER 33

*S*arah and Noah sat in the Adirondack chairs in the backyard while Nathalie, Ben and Johnny played.

"That was fantastic. Thank you for asking us over for dinner." Noah smiled.

"You're welcome. I'm glad I'm finally able to make something edible for a change." She massaged her shoulder. "Oh, I meant to tell you, you were right."

He frowned. "About what?"

"I took your suggestion and brought donuts to the teachers last week. They loved it. Even Carol seemed almost pleasant."

"Glad to hear it." Noah smiled.

"Even Milly seems to be warming up to me. Which is a miracle in itself. I'm thinking of taking Johnny back to church Sunday. He mentioned how much he missed his Sunday School teacher."

"Why don't you ride with us?"

She nodded. "I think I'll take you up on it."

"Good, thanks by the way for taking Nathalie shopping. I have no idea what little girls wear these days."

"Anytime. I love shopping." She'd taken Nathalie shopping for some new clothes a few days ago when she needed some summer clothes. She volunteered to take the little girl, and Noah joyfully relented.

"How's work?" Noah asked.

"It's work. It puts food on the table and keeps the bills paid. I go clock in, sort the mail and clock out."

He frowned. "You don't exactly seem to love it."

She shrugged. "Who really loves their job?"

Noah studied her. "I would love it if you did. I mean, since you've been working at the post office, you seem a little...down."

"Really?" She sighed heavily. She'd finally gotten to the point where she had let go of the bitterness of giving her inheritance, and in essence, her dream away. "I would say I'm content."

He frowned. "It feels like you've settled. That's different from being content. And you are not the kind of person who can live like that."

Silence stretched between them.

"I meant to tell you I saw your uncle..."

"Here?" She straightened in her seat. "He's not allowed to be anywhere near us or Hopeton."

He narrowed his eyes. "I was going to say I saw him when he was leaving town. He was getting gas when I pulled in to the gas station. He looked like he was in a hurry and said very little. I noticed he had a large bag of money on the passenger's seat. I tried calling you, but you never answered so I called your attorney."

Her eyes widened.

"Don't worry. Mr. Willard was very selective about what he told me. I asked if Oliver had robbed a bank. He said no. He said he had robbed you. He told me to call Mrs. Hadley at CPS and ask her what was going on."

"She didn't tell you, did she?"

"She's my mom's cousin. Legally, no she can't say anything. But between you and me, yes, she said your uncle made a false claim about you and your parenting skills. I put two and two together and figured you paid him to leave. Is that right?"

She nodded once.

"And I'm guessing you paid him with your inheritance."

She sighed heavily. "I had no other choice."

"I need to tell you something."

"What?" She looked at him.

"I'm sorry I didn't listen to you when you said you had doubts about Oliver. You were right, and I was wrong."

She shifted in her seat. "You never said why you were calling this morning." She quickly changed the subject.

"Well, I wanted to talk to you about something."

"Okay."

"Remember when I videoed you singing your song?"

"Yeah, you sent it to me to see if I wanted to make changes. Why?"

"Well, one of my clients had a brother who is in the music business. He put me in contact with him."

She held her breath.

"I don't want you to be mad or anything. I know I should have asked your permission first, but I went ahead and sent it to him."

"You did?" She blinked and bolted up straight.

"And he liked it. He liked it a lot. He said you are incredibly talented singer and songwriter. He wants to meet with you to offer you a contract."

She jumped up and screamed. Then reality came crashing down around her. She eased back into her seat. "I can't accept a contract. I can't go all the way to Hollywood. I have to stay here with Johnny."

"I explained your situation to him. He understands. He actually has a home in Nashville which wouldn't be that big of a drive. He said you could come down to his home in Tennessee and stay with his family, or if you'd rather park your van on his land, you can do that. He was very fascinated by the fact you remodeled a van."

"But what about my job?"

"Sarah, he sent a contract to me to give to you. It's a nice contract. For that one song alone you would make four times what your parents left you."

"What?" He eyes widened.

"He says he understands that you are raising your brother. He said that you don't have to tour right away. He said to come down to his home as soon as school is out and bring Johnny. You guys record songs for a few weeks, and then you come back home. Your record won't be released until next year. In the meantime, you can write songs and build up inventory for when you are ready to record. Or, you can sell the songs your write. It seems you have a lot of choices about your future. "

She shook her head. Tears welled up behind her eyes, streaming down her face. "I can't believe this is happening. I can't."

Noah walked over to her and knelt in front of her. "I can. I always knew you were going to be special. I knew your dreams would come true."

She reached out and touched his face. "Noah, I'm going to kiss you."

He smiled. "Those are words I've been waiting to hear for ten years."

When their lips met, joy and elation washed over her. Her heart jolted with a spark.

"Eww."

They pulled apart to see Nathalie and Johnny giving them looks of disgust.

"So does this mean you two are getting married?" Nathalie brightened. Johnny didn't look that thrilled.

Sarah looked at Noah who went red with embarassment.

She smiled. "I think we should just start with a date. And then see how it goes from there."

Sarah looked back at the man who had just changed her life and had never let her give up on her dreams.

She didn't think she was the marrying type, but Noah Wellington, might just have changed her mind.

ABOUT THE AUTHOR

Jodi Allen Brice is an USA Today best-selling author of over thirty novels. She had written several series under Jodi Allen Brice and you can find more information about her latest release on her website
http://jodiallenbrice.com

Book 1

Book 2

Book 3

Printed in Great Britain
by Amazon

21891950R00118